INNKEEPER

JOURNAL DISCOVERED: REVEALING 'TORTURE MURDERS' & ATROCITIES

By DR. C.E. GRENCI

CONTENTS

DISCLAIMER i

COPYRIGHT ii

DEDICATION iii

AUTHOR'S PREVIEW iv

AUTHOR'S WARNING & RATING vi

ANDREW WEBB'S PROLOGUE vii

CHAPTER 1 EARLY YEARS 8

CHAPTER 2 FUNERAL HOME FOLLIES 12

CHAPTER 3 MANHOOD VS. DEATH 15

CHAPTER 4 SCHOOL DAZE 18

CHAPTER 5 HEROIN VS. SANITY 21

CHAPTER 6 FADED FANTASIES 23

CHAPTER 7 THE CRIMINAL MIND 26

CHAPTER 8 INFAMOUS SERIAL KILLERS 30

CHAPTER 9 NECK-TIE STRANGLER 32

CHAPTER 10 DOUBLE LIFE OF CRIME 37

CHAPTER 11 INNKEEPER VS. UNDERTAKER 40

CHAPTER 12 SINISTER TALES OF LOVE & DEATH 45

CHAPTER 13 DESIGNING A 'HOUSE OF HORRORS' 54

   MANSION'S - 1ST FLOOR FAÇADE & DÉCOR 55

   ASYLUM - 2ND FLOOR LUNACY 57

   SANCTUARY + 3RD FLOOR GUEST ROOMS 60

   DEVIL'S DUNGEON - BASEMENT 61

CHAPTER 14 PAULINE'S DISTURBING DIARY 63

CHAPTER 15 ANDREW'S VIEW OF PAULINE'S DIARY 70

CHAPTER 16 PREDISPOSED TO BE A 'SADIST' 72

CHAPTER 17 INNKEEPER'S FORMAL FASHION & ETIQUETTE 74

CHAPTER 18 ANDREW'S FATEFUL FLASHBACK 76

CHAPTER 19 WELCOME-BLUE PINE GUEST INN 77

CHAPTER 20 AGONY & ECSTACY HOMICIDES 2ND FLOOR 79

    Room 201 - H.H. Holmes' Gas Chamber 79

    Room 203 - Electric Lounge 81

    Room 205 – Medieval Fair 86

    Room 207 – Dark Carnival 88

    Room 209 – Blue Pine Zoo 96

AUTHOR'S WARNING FOR 99

'SATAN'S PLAYGROUND' 99

    Room 211 – Satan's Playground 100

    Room 213 - Coffin Chaos 104

    Room 215 – 'Bettie Page' Dive 110

    Room 217 – Victorian Brothel 115

    Room 219 – Necktie Party 122

    Devil's Dungeon - Postmortem 126

CHAPTER 21 ELLA & FOUR ROSES 130

CHAPTER 22 INNKEEPER'S CRUEL COURTSHIP 134

CHAPTER 23 A BLESSING VS. A CURSE 139

CHAPTER 24 BETRAYAL & BLISS.................................... 140

CHAPTER 25 VICTORIAN FUNERAL................................ 145

CHAPTER 26 ENGLISH TEA PARTY 148

CHAPTER 27 INNKEEPER'S MOCK MARRIAGE 152

CHAPTER 28 HONEYMOON TO DIE FOR 153

CHAPTER 29 ANDREW'S WEB 155

CHAPTER 30 'PILLOW TALK' IN THE MORGUE 158

CHAPTER 31 BLUE PINE'S 'FOREVER' KEEPSAKES 160

CHAPTER 32 INNKEEPER'S NIGHTMARE 162

CHAPTER 33 THE PERFECT STORM 166

CHAPTER 34 INNKEEEEPER VS. PROFESSOR 169

CHAPTER 35 ANDREW WEBB'S TESTAMENT 172

CHAPTER 36 THE DEAD END 175

THE LETTER 179

GLOSSARY 182

ABOUT THE AUTHOR - BIO 192

FOLLOW THE AUTHOR 193

AUTHOR'S BOOKS 195

Links - To Author's Books 196

PHOTO - DR. C.E. GRENCI 198

DISCLAIMER

The story in this book is a work of creative fiction. The names and identifying details of the individuals are fictitious. In all instances, the essence of the story's dialogue and drama is fiction. This book contains graphic sexual scenes, extreme torture, murder, death and sensitive subject matter suitable for mature, open-minded readers eighteen years and older.

COPYRIGHT

Copyright © 2025 Dr. Charlayne Grenci

DEDICATION

Seril L. Grossfeld, Esq.

Writing the 'Innkeeper' has been a dedication to a time-consuming project for over a year. Seril has been my devoted and loyal partner for thirty-two years. With Seril's constant care, encouragement and love, I have always had the necessary backing, time and freedom to pursue my education, my other professions and to continue my profession as a published author.

Without Seri's strength, immense support, counsel and understanding, my extraordinary retirement years and the comfortable, fun-loving lifestyle she provides would not have been possible. For all this, I truly thank my dearest Seril with endless gratitude, love and respect. ~ Dr. C.E. Grenci

AUTHOR'S PREVIEW

Andrew Webb is the Innkeeper. He is a mastermind with advanced mental acuity and genius intelligence. He is also the personification of evil, madness, and a man without a soul. He is a ruthless, violent murderer who someday may be reputed as America's most brutal, deranged, infamous, serial killer of all time. Consequently, his notoriety belongs with other ill-famed American killers such as H.H. Holmes, Ted Bundy, Gary Ridgway, Jeffrey Dahmer, David Parker Ray and British killers Jack the Ripper and John Christie, just to name a few.

Andrew Webb had a few of his own unique, vile and disturbing individualities which were unlike any of the others, yet he did possess some similar behaviors to a few. Andrew's exclusive complexity, duality, irresistible charm, and classical manner put him at the top of the list or in a class by himself. In fact, from one perspective, Mr. Webb's profile encompasses a strange and uncommon combination of several serial killers which is learned by the entrees in his personal journal. Most serial killers operate with the same or similar routine with each kill. But Andrew Webb was an exception. He cleverly and consciously deceived law enforcement for decades by not adhering to the same modus operandi from one killing to the next.

In conclusion, Andrew Webb is a charming, handsome monster, a full-time psychopath and devoted predator whose life from childhood to adulthood was disturbing, bizarre and unimaginable. This book, which was compiled from Andrew's journal, will be a good read for psychologists, forensic pathologists, law enforcement, mental health professionals and all individuals who are interested in what really goes on behind closed doors and what goes on in the minds of some killers. This book delves deeper into the dark abyss where most authors, guest speakers and journalists don't dare to tread. However, I have no problem putting in print the reality of a killer's worst dirty dees and describing those atrocities in precise detail. This book isn't reading material or entertainment for most readers.

Personally, I always seek literature and research that ignites my deepest emotions and stimulates my creative imagination to excessive depth and challenge. When I read, I expect to be shocked or captivated by a theme which inspires my desire and expectation. I must find the source of my reading material suspenseful, entertaining, educational or captivating.

On that same note, as an author, I find it necessary to arouse the same emotions in my readers. I strive to evoke sheer excitement and anticipation or make you uncomfortable with fear, violence and the bizarre. I assure you 'Innkeeper' will trigger your deepest emotions and arouse more than your curiosity. In truth, the fiction in this book is based on similar historical facts that have proven serial killers are constantly lurking and hunting in our society's mainstream. ~ Dr. C. E. Grenci

AUTHOR'S WARNING & RATING

'Innkeeper' is bizarre, disturbing, shocking and taboo on many levels. The contents contain extreme, unimaginable, illegal criminal behavior and monstrous methods of torture. Some readers may define the confessions of Webb's nefarious activities in this journal illegal, immoral, graphically evil and/or obscene. Therefore, if obscenity, sadism and sexual graphic literature offend you or is against your moral code, this read is not for you. If you choose to continue, read at your own risk with free will and an open mind. 'Obscene' is in the eyes of the beholder. The author will take no responsibility for those who perceive this content to be obscene.

This book is Rated: NC-17 – Adults Only.

Not recommended for readers under 18.

ANDREW WEBB'S

PROLOGUE

My Journal is a hardcore, dark and gritty account of what I do and how well I do it, detail by gritty and vile detail. If you choose to read my journal, or endure my journal out of curiosity, be prepared to have a front seat as a voyeur and a witness to a plethora of evils you have never imagined existed. You will read about the sordid and sinister thoughts inside the demented mind of a prolific murderer. You will observe atrocities like no other serial murderer. You will be the judge and jury. Would you condemn me to a violent death, too? I've been doomed since childhood. If authorities ever find my secret property with these confessions while I'm alive, my capture would surely be a televised, high profile court case because I'm your next-door nightmare. I'm the bad man your mother warned you about. Welcome to my sick and wacky world. This is me.

My name is Webb. ~ Andrew Webb.

Quote: "I am under no obligation to make sense to you."

~ Mad Hatter.

CHAPTER 1

EARLY YEARS

At the curious age of six, my father took me downstairs to the basement for the first time to see where he worked every day, often late into the night. It was a creepy, dark room with a bad smell, then Dad turned on a light above a gruesome sight. On a shiny, cold, metal embalming table, I saw a lifeless body lying in an unzipped, black body bag with glassy eyes halfway open and a jaw hanging down. For most children, that would be frightening. Dad thought it would shock me, but it didn't faze me much at all. I remember his weird expression when I did not turn to run. I eagerly asked him unexpected questions about the wrinkled skin on the formidable corpse, because I had never seen a dead person. I think he had hoped I would be afraid to ever return to the basement, but alternatively, that first trip to the embalming room had peaked my morbid curiosity to a point I was not aware of at the time.

Dad explained that this old lady, Mrs. Martin, was eighty-five years old and she had just died in a fatal car crash. Her pale, wrinkled face was disfigured, and the left side of her face was caved in with an eyeball smeared on her cheek like a blue yolk fried egg. Her once neatly combed and permed, silvery, white hair was full of crusted blood. Mrs. Martin's empty eye socket made her look like a monster, but that didn't scare me either. Dad said she was pronounced dead at the scene of the accident and was taken by ambulance to the nearby hospital and put into their morgue until her daughter arrived. She identified her mother and requested her remains be taken immediately to this funeral home where they had done family business before. Dad also warned me not to get spooked because sometimes cadavers that have died a violent death like Mrs. Martin might move, twitch or make a disturbing noise such as a groan, squeak, grunt or fart, so I was expecting to experience more. Grandma Martin smelled putrid because of the urine and feces she was laying in, in the coroner's body bag. That was the gross part for me.

What my dad said next, I wasn't prepared for. He told me to touch Mrs. Martin's body to feel the lifelike warmth that still lingered, and not to be afraid of the dead because they cannot hurt you. I hesitated, so dad took my right hand and placed it on the dead woman's bloody forearm and proceeded to run my hand along her arm in a stroking fashion. Then he said to me,

"Son, you see there's nothing to be afraid of, is there? She can't feel you." I didn't answer right away, so dad continued.

"Sometimes, I find fascinating cadavers put on this table from car accidents, heart attacks or freak accidents. I don't favor the suicide or drowned victims or any other cold ones that have had an autopsy." I asked my dad what he meant by fascinating cadavers but didn't expect his truthful answer. He explained,

"Andrew, you're not old enough to understand what I'm about to tell you. The only reason I will tell you is because you showed no fear of this disfigured corpse and at your youthful age, that's extraordinary. You see my boy, I'm attracted to young, pretty girls, preferably warm, underage pretty girls and that's against the law. If I engage in that behavior and get caught, I'll end up in prison, so, I thought of another way to satisfy my deviant desires."

I asked what his deviant desires were, not knowing the big words. At this point, I was almost seven years old. I wanted to hear more. Why? I didn't have a clue, but I had always been a curious child. Dad told mum that extreme curiosity from a child so young was a sign of above average intelligence. I told dad to continue, and he anxiously obliged.

"Son, you may have already noticed dead people arrive with a horrible odor. that will stay in your memory forever. Death also has a repulsive smell when a body begins to decompose, a smell no one can forget. To me it smells like rotten cabbage, but other people describe it differently. Soon, you will notice Rigor Mortis with Mrs. Martin, maybe in another hour or so. Later, I will explain to you the four stages of putrefaction. I won't go into that now, but I'll just tell you, dead bodies eventually turn black. That's enough. Tonight, I will tell you more about... ah, more about me.

Andrew, this secret is private between you and me. Your mum, nor the owner of this house of death cannot learn of my secret. I'm warning you, if either of them gets a whiff of this, I'll lose my job here, our family will lose our lodging and my prudish, religious wife, your darling, doting mother, will divorce me! I'm counting on you to understand how serious my secret is. Ok? Do we have a deal? Do you promise to never say a word to anyone, son?"

Dad, stood stiff, staring me straight in the eyes waiting for a quick response, but I was temporarily stunned by hearing my father's concern. Euw, yeh. He wanted me to assume the responsibility of retaining the knowledge of a serious secret. I stood frozen in time, and speechless for a quick pause to digest his significant request. I swallowed deeply, bit my lip, and responded, OK, dad. He kept his wide-open eyes glued to mine and cocked his head to the side like he was deciding whether to trust me. He made a weird gesture with his mouth, drawing back his lips with a big hiss and inhaling followed by a loud exhale. Then dad made an about face and walked three steps away before turning around to face me. Nervously, clenching his fists with a grimaced expression, dad spoke.

"Andrew, I'm sexually attracted to deceased girls, only if they are young, pretty and still warm. Like I said before, I don't favor cold ones. Tried it but…, I know this doesn't make sense to you, but select, warm cadavers are a turn on for me. Explanation and reasoning would sound sick to anyone else, but when they're dead I can do whatever I want with their beautiful, soft, sometimes virgin bodies. Never any complaints or resistance. I have full control. I like that. After doing that once, which was several years ago, I was hooked and then the occasional sex with your mum didn't feel good at all, besides it had never been great anyway. Your mum always complained and rejected me most of the time, which is why warm, silent corpses became desirable. I am determined to continue working at this funeral home for that reason. I'll admit, I became obsessed, or whatever you want to call it and suddenly I couldn't control my abnormal appetite for sweet, soft & quiet female bodies.

Perhaps you'll understand one day. I know I shouldn't have told you any of this, but it appears I desperately needed to share with someone I can trust and have an outlet. It's frustrating and mind-boggling at times when you know you're all alone in a perverted, alternative world. But it's my choice."

I didn't understand everything that eerie evening in the morgue, but I learned years later that my dad wasn't a normal man, and with the knowledge and exposure he bestowed on me at such a young age, I was headed for a bizarre career and lifestyle myself. Like father, like son?

My parents didn't know I had killed two of the neighborhood alley cats when I was about five. Those were strange experiences, but for some reason I enjoyed it. There was something interesting about watching life leave the felines while I was choaking them to death. Maybe I became curious about death and experimenting with death because I was born in an environment immersed in death. The typical, frequent conversations I overheard growing up in a funeral home, were mostly about corpses, death and activities in the morgue. Now, dad has exposed me to a whole new world for my anxious, aberrant mind to explore. Dad couldn't have guessed he had poured fuel on an existing fire. At seven years old, right or wrong, I was already way ahead of my peers in knowledge and life experiences.

Quote: "Children are completely egoistic: they feel their needs intensely and strive ruthlessly to satisfy them."

~ Sigmund Freud – Physician & Pioneer Psychoanalyst

CHAPTER 2

FUNERAL HOME FOLLIES

A few years went by, and I had entered puberty at ten, sooner than most of the other boys at school. By the age of twelve, I was still doing well in school and had been hanging out with dad more when he was in the preparation room. The more I saw, the more curious I became. My classmates thought I was weird by merely living at a funeral home. If they knew my thoughts and fantasies, I would surely be ostracized by most of them, excluding a male student or two that had a hunger for guts, gore and horror. My appetite and expectations for more were increasing at a rapid pace. Every evening after homework, I was excited to join Dad in the basement. The morgue, I call it, had become my favorite space in the house, possibly my preferred place anywhere.

Once, I put my finger in an old man's mouth, but that felt cold and sticky. Yuck. Another time, when Dad had run to the bathroom, I put my finger inside a female corpse's vagina. I think she was about Mum's age. It was still warm and slippery, but my finger smelled gross, like rotten onions, so I wasn't going to ever do that again. Never. I didn't know if that unexpected finding would affect my heterosexuality in a negative way. I wasn't too young to realize all this morgue exposure and my willing participation had already caused a significant, detrimental effect on my sexuality. Imagine being more comfortable in a morgue with dead people than spending time with the living. That was me at twelve. I will gladly continue documenting more madness at the miserable house of death.

Our most recent deceased guest was brought in on a rainy, miserable afternoon. She was a seventeen-year-old female. The name on her big toe, toe tag said Jackie Hill, date of her death and a case number. I asked Dad what happened to her. The medical examiner told him she was riding in the car with her father, who was speeding in his yellow, 1923 Duesenberg Model A. He lost control on a sharp curve and wrapped his precious car around an electric pole going 70 mph. The impact killed Mr. Hill, his daughter and their Boston Terrier instantaneously. The police requested an autopsy from Mr. Hill because they found an opened, broken bottle of Cutty Sark on the floorboard. Jackie and her puppy were thrown from the convertible. The accident report stated Mr. Hill was crushed beyond recognition, his torso was completely embedded into the steering wheel, and his head had been decapitated by the big engine. The rescue team found the remains of his skull yards away with a metal rod stuffed through his jaw. They said it was the most gruesome sight they had ever seen.

Our pretty little friend here was killed when her body was ejected and went airborne just far enough to have landed on her back on top of a spiked fence. The wrought iron spikes severed her spinal cord in several places, from neck to sacroiliac and ripped apart her vital organs. Dad went on to further explain.

"Andrew, unfortunately, we will end up having to retrieve Mr. Hill's corpse from the hospital morgue after his autopsy. That my son isn't going to be pleasant. A closed casket if there's a funeral, and cremation is all we can do for him. I hope the family requests an urn instead of a casket.

On a higher note, I was thrilled to see little Jackie received no injuries to her face or breasts. Son, take your first look at what I fancy."

Dad got visibly nervous and aroused as he abruptly pulled the red stained sheet down off Jackie's face and torso to show me how attractive she was with her long, blonde, tangled hair and large, milky breasts sticking out of her torn, bloody blouse. I was thinking, ah, ok, Dad, but I knew he wanted me to agree, so I agreed she looked good except for her crystal blue eyes half open that appeared to be staring at the ceiling. I preferred closed eyes. There was a stream of blood that had trickled out of the corners of her mouth, down the side of her blushed cheeks that had pooled near her clavicle. I remember thinking what a damned shame. In a couple of years, I would have dated that sweet patootie.

After dad washed and disinfected Julie's corpse, he removed her personal items and worked on the teenager's chart. Then he announced he would take a brief break to have slugburgers and beer with Mum upstairs. I was surprised he left me alone to do some sweeping and cleaning before he returned to finish his night's work with the new corpse. I estimated he'd be upstairs for about thirty minutes, so I did my chores faster than ever before because my curiosity had risen to a pinnacle. I was worried my snooping would get me into trouble with Dad, but my desire to experiment took priority over my better sense. I didn't know a damned thing about having sex with a girl, but tonight I was eager to find out what it was like on my own. I had been conveniently bestowed some private time with this lovely dame, but I wasn't sure if I should risk being caught. I gambled. I turned out the main overhead light and just relied on the matches I had in my pocket. I figured I'd been given a rare opportunity to try something different. I knew before twelve there was something wrong with me. What twelve-year-old wants to have sex with a cadaver, pretty or not? Ugh. I quickly lit the first match and observed Jackie's body from head to toe, just to get a good look where everything was before the match went out. Poof. Now, I had to navigate in the dark remembering what I saw.

I had been having nocturnal emissions since about ten and I had a decent size boner for my age, compared to other students in the boys' locker room, but never had any kind of sex with a girl. None of my classmates had experienced anything more than masturbating either. I had been masturbating at least twice a day for more than two years and tonight I felt like doing more than that. I had been getting aroused while watching Dad work on young female cadavers for a few years. He let me touch them all over, but he never encouraged anything more. Tonight was the perfect time to start seeking experience on my own, alone. Alone. At last alone with a pretty one.

CHAPTER 3

MANHOOD VS. DEATH

I slipped the white sheet up to the cadaver's neck and stood at the foot of the embalming table for a couple of minutes contemplating my next move knowing my time was limited. I spread Jackie's feet wide apart and stared at the little pink bean slightly peeking out of Jackie's lower lips. I noticed she must have trimmed the blonde hair around her quim because most other cadavers that came through our door had a hairy, nasty smelling growler. That's why I had made up my mind I would never entertain the idea of an Aussie kiss or put my nose near a lady's crotch area. I saw that Jackie had beautiful, turquoise blue eyes peeping out of her half-closed eye lids. I became transfixed on them for a moment as I had never seen eyes that color before, but I had to close them before anything else. I gently ran my fingertips down over her eyelids and closed them.

After three long minutes of nervous contemplation, I pulled myself up onto the cold metal table and unzipped my fly for the first time other than to urinate or undress. I knelt between Julie's thighs and used my fingers to caress her warm abdomen, then her private area which was almost bare. Oddly enough, this exploration wasn't a turn off for me and my sausage reached full attention on its own. Dad had told me to refer to my member as a hot dog which is what they called penises in his time, but I preferred sausage because mine was extra-large for my age. I spread open her pretty quim like it was beckoning a visit from my nervous fingertips, lowered my torso and for the first time, I thrust all 7 inches of my naughty-bits straight into her dark, wet cavern. It didn't take more than three hard thrusts synchronizing with my swollen hot bollocks banging against her bum before I emptied an ample load into the dead cadaver. A tidal wave of novel pleasure and relief swooped over me, and my body shook like it had never done before. Was this a good thing or was this the beginning of a more sinister future for me? I remember thinking when I regained full consciousness, would I get hooked on this form of sexual activity or was this just a one-time fling into a forbidden, ultimate ecstasy?

I was kneeling between this beautiful creature's thin, limp legs, feeling lightheaded, and satisfied but confused and a bit humiliated. I felt like I was going to pass out and topple over on top of her. I took a deep breath, pinched my arm, and slapped my face to reclaim awareness and control. Then, I started to move slowly backwards to the edge of the table, but I was so weak and spent that I collapsed on top of this cadaver named Jackie, with my face ending up between her pert baps. Stunned, I lay there for a couple of minutes enjoying the feeling of her warm flesh hugging each side of my face. The sweet smell of her body's sweat filled my virgin nostrils and rushed to my brain like a snort of heroin. I laid there dazed on that soft, human pillow until I had enough energy and motivation to remove myself from the most compromising situation, I had ever been in. I was ashamed of my disrespectful conduct towards a corpse, someone's daughter, maybe someone's girlfriend, but I was also reveling in the experience I just had. By the way, I tend to revert to my British slang when I talk about intimate sex. As I slid down off Jackie's body, I felt uneasy like something was wrong.

Little did I know, Dad had been standing in the hall watching me through the door's tiny window for my entire performance. I literally got caught with my pants down. When Dad said my name, I almost fell, trying to pull up my pants while jumping down off the table backwards. In the process, I slammed my deflating stiff against the hard edge of the cold stainless steel. Oh my God, that hurt, that snapped me back to reality instantaneously. I didn't know whether to turn around and face my dad, so I swiftly stuffed my piece back into my pants, zipped it halfway up and quickly turned around with wild eyes, a red, distorted face, and a pounding heart. We stared at each other for about thirty seconds and then Dad spoke first. I was in shock, embarrassed and thoroughly speechless.

"Andrew, it's ok, son. Don't be embarrassed in front of your good ole' dad. I was wondering if you were ever going to take a poke at one of those babes. How was it, son?"

It felt like my lips were glued together. I was afraid to say the wrong thing and I did.

"Dad," I said breathing heavily,

"It was ok. Not what I expected. Do you do this, dad? Is this what you were hinting at years ago?"

"Between you and me only, son, yes. Ever since your mum had you, her body changed so much, and then you received most of her attention. I took a stab at this for the first time about twelve years ago and liked it. I didn't think of it as cheating on your mum 'cause I didn't have to pay for it and the dame was deceased. The opportunity presented itself occasionally which was often enough for me because I don't require sex too often. Your mum had a lot to do with that."

Dad stood in front of me with a peculiar look on his face while he confessed, but it made me feel better. Like father, like son, I thought, as I quickly passed by my authoritative figure and hurried out of the embalming room. I headed for my bedroom to clean up and change clothes. Since Dad had been doing this for so many years, not needing sex from a live woman which I figured was abnormal sexual behavior, so I gave up feeling guilty and ashamed of myself.

CHAPTER 4

SCHOOL DAZE

I wondered why I never heard any gory gossip from fellow students in high school, but then their fathers didn't work at a funeral home. I always felt like a complete, unwelcome outsider until I stood in at one of my classmates' circle jerks. I was the boy who was more confident and quite proud because I was pleasantly surprised to see I was bigger than all of them. Behind closed doors, I may have earned a bit of respect because a couple of them were frequently asking how my banana was hanging.

Occasionally, circle jerks took place under the grandstands behind our high school where the upper classmen played football in the afternoons. My classmates always talked to girls in their classes and talked about them in dirty ways but never about dead bodies. When they talked in front of me, I would fantasize about a pretty, young cadaver still warm on the embalming table.

One early evening when the lads and I were about to engage in our monthly jerk off party under the grandstands, two young, rich girls showed up under the grandstands to watch. They were both students in my classes, about my age, and their parents were prominent and well-known in town. The girl with curly black hair and braces appeared reticent to come in close. Charlie, who was the bold and forward boy in my school, was a few years older than me. Abruptly, he stuffed his member into his pants and left our circle to go talk to the girls. He urged the two brunette beauties to join us for a little fun and assured them they were safe; they wouldn't get hurt, and no one would tell on them. At this time, the curly headed girl turned spontaneously, almost running into me and ran away as fast as her tiny feet would take her, out from under the grandstands and off across the field towards the residential area where she must have lived. The other girl, Linda, with thick brunette braids across pinned across the top of her head, wearing lipstick, a short skirt, and white pumps. Within minutes, Charlie had convinced Linda, who had brought her dog, to go over to a corner with him and remove her clothing, which she did without reservation. I wanted to shout out to the naïve, gullible girl not to undress, and to run away like her friend did. If she only knew what was going to happen, it would not be a pleasurable experience for her, not to mention it would ruin her reputation. I couldn't control the situation, so I just stood there still as a statue and watched what played out. Charlie didn't waste any time taking control and full advantage of the thirteen-year-old girl. I wanted to run away myself, but my feet felt glued to the cement floor. I wanted to watch but I knew I shouldn't be there. What happened next was a sin and a shame for that girl's high society family.

Charlie took off all his clothes and swiftly laid Linda down on the floor on his clothes and pinned her wrists against the cement floor over her head. Linda burst out crying, begging him to stop and get off her, but Charlie didn't listen or care, he was on a mission and going to do what he wanted to do. The petite junior high student was no match for Charlie's jock strength and determination. He told her to shut up, or he'd kill her little dog that was shaking with fear for her owner. This is how it went.

"I'm begging you, get off me, please get off me!" Charlie took one hand and tightly covered Linda's mouth and said,

"I told you to shut your mouth, bitch, or I will get up and kill that no-good canine of yours! What a pathetic excuse for a dog. I'm going to take my hand off your mouth, but you better be quiet, you little whore!" Charlie took his right hand off his victim's mouth and grabbed his penis to force into her tight, virgin womanhood.

"No, don't do this! Stop! It hurts! Please… (crying out loud), I don't want this. Stop it!" Charlie wasn't paying any attention to his young victim. He spit his hand, rubbed it into her vagina with his fingers, then with a hard thrust he roughly shoved himself through her fragile hymen. Linda screamed out in pain. All I could think was, she was lucky Charlie had a tiny pole. I don't think mine would have fit.

"Ahhh! Stop this and get off me!" But her screams soon softened, and she fainted from the brutal experience and pain. The high school jock engaged in copulation for only a few intense strokes until he spilled his fresh seeds straight down into her uninvited space. I was thinking that innocent little girl could end up pregnant. I wondered if I was going to be asked to be a witness of this rape. I didn't know if I wouldn't rat on Charlie because I had my own dark side. I knew what he did to that young, impressionable girl would mark her for life. It was cruel, brutal, and illegal. I knew it was wrong, but I felt no empathy for the girl. No emotions. None.

After graduating high school, I went to the NYU School of Medicine for only two years and became interested in becoming a medical examiner. I dropped out two years shy of getting a bachelor's degree because my freedom was too limited; it conflicted with my potent sexual desires. However, during those two years I spent extra time in the library doing research on sex and sexual perversions. It wasn't until then that I learned about necrophilia, 'which is a sexual attraction to dead bodies.' That's not the clinical definition but it was obviously what my father and I enjoyed. What we do has occurred throughout history, that's all I have to say.

I was compelled to write a little background on my childhood so my adulthood might be better understood. Not seeking approval, none the less shocking, but maybe more understandable, especially with psychologists and the like. My life from the age of five to twelve years old was unlike most boys my age. Was I predisposed to becoming a monster?

CHAPTER 5

HEROIN VS. SANITY

Nontraditional sex wasn't the only thing I learned from Dad when I was a youngster. He told me he ordered heroin kits frequently from the Sears & Roebuck catalog. He didn't tell me about his addiction until I graduated high school. I suppose he thought if I knew about his secret sex habit and I had already been initiated into his forbidden world of necrophilia, then I was man enough to know about his other bad habit.

Mr. Andrew Webb, Sr., my father, told me that doing heroin made it more tolerable to deal with cadavers, bloody disfigured accident victims and other horrible-looking corpses. Plus, he said doing the drug helped mitigate his guilt for his sexual desire for dead bodies. He also told me his heroin use helped to desensitize him from all his inner demons. He said he had become a careful but frequent user shortly after I was born, and that was another secret he kept from Elizabeth, my mum. I understood why he led a double life because of mum. I realized at a young age why dad needed frequent but temporary escapes from the reality of his occupation, the ways of his life and the ways of his wife. Mrs. Webb could drive anyone batty with her overbearing religious beliefs and bossy attitude. That's why I started at a young age to spend my free time with Dad in the basement after school and after homework.

Dad pulled out his drug kit from its hiding place to show me that same night he confessed about it. He told me heroin was a modified form of morphine, and an opioid. He offered me some and explained I would feel an intense pleasurable feeling; a strong increase in euphoria with a warm flush sensation that would last a few minutes, which would be followed by a sedation that would last for a few hours. That night, with Dad's permission and supervision, was the first time I tried heroin. I can't deny I liked it.

From seventeen on, I engaged in a couple of bad habits. My father was my role model, my influencer and enabler, so whatever he thought was acceptable behavior, I followed suit and by my eighteenth birthday, I was trying to escape from my inner demons with heroin, sometimes with Dad in the embalming room and sometimes alone in my room. A 'sniff before a stiff' we often whispered to each other with a light chuckle afterwards. I agreed the deadly substance did make a big difference in coping with everything that plagued me, the voices in my head and it gave me a marvelous high.

On Q, we both stood behind the locked door in the embalming area, and took a hit before working together on a body with extreme, grotesque injuries. Other times, we sniffed before we took turns raping a new corpse that arrived, sometimes looking better than most living females, in our eyes only. The heroin helped me through my feelings of guilt and new temptations to go hunting. In a short time, I became as dependent on heroin as Mr. Webb, Sr. Now we were partners, sharing two big secrets we dared not share with anyone else. That became our strong bond. Mum was so into her church, Bible and wifely domestic duties, she was too occupied, brainwashed and blinded by religion to ever find out.

Quote: "Religion is comparable to a child's neurosis. The whole thing is so patently infantile. So foreign to reality, that to anyone with a friendly attitude to humanity it is painful to think that the great majority of mortals will never be able to rise above this view of life." ~ Sigmund Freud

Physician & Pioneer Psychoanalyst

CHAPTER 6

FADED FANTASIES

Our family stayed employed, living at the funeral home in New York for another few years. After high school graduation, I attended New York University (NYU). My goal for a bachelor's degree included courses in mortuary science, criminology, anatomy, forensic pathology, and chemistry. I had a full 5 course load for two reasons. I wanted to work in a county morgue, not a funeral home, plus, I needed to have a backup of education if my double life went south in the future. During my four years at NYU, I communicated from home which was difficult, but in my mind, I had no choice. Occasionally, I stayed overnight in the big city at an old hotel near the school. It was there, I had my first experience hunting, going to the red-light district to pick up a prostitute. There were several locations associated with illicit activities in the city, so over those four years I didn't have to go to the same place twice.

I picked up my first victim in an area called The Tenderloin, in Manhattan on 42nd Street where I was also introduced to porn shops, peep shows and a variety of decadent places I had never seen. I had a rude awakening and an alternative education that first year at school. I wasn't close to any fellow students, but I heard the word of where to go to get most anything.

I'll never forget Sheila, my first live victim and 42nd Street prostitute. She guided me to a dark, vacant alley a few blocks away. I gave her $20, then told her to lay down on the front seat on her stomach, in the pretense I was going to have bum sex with her. She wasn't in favor of this position, but I calmly assured her it was good. I strangled her with the tie I was wearing. It took a few minutes to be sure she wasn't breathing, then I went to the passenger side door, turned her body over and pulled her lifeless body to the edge of the seat so I could shag her. I don't have to penetrate my victim. I was satisfied just stroking it against her thighs. In 30 seconds or less when that was over, I anxiously tore a nylon off her left leg and threw her body out of my car. I had deposited a fair share of semen on the corpse, tucked her nylon in my trousers pockets and fled feeling a different sort of high than heroin or cadavers.

I sped away into the depth of the night, back to my hotel room to have a snack and to study into the wee hours. I frequently sniffed the black, silky nylon and got aroused repeatedly which distracted me by reliving the first-time hunting success again. Eventually, after I was totally spent, I resumed my studies. It had been a thrilling but terrifying experience wondering if anyone got a glimpse of my car leaving the scene. I learned that night, I had immensely enjoyed strangling the pathetic whore with my necktie. I thoroughly enjoyed the anticipation and challenge of the hunt and killing a live female. It was a definite power and control experience, a novel one for me.

After that first encounter, I took a long break from hunting and concentrated exclusively on my courses. Naturally, I used that nylon frequently during the long break and masturbated to that fantasy to blow off frustration. I will always take a souvenir from the scene of my crimes to better remember the victim and the experience. A personal item from my victim also gives me a sense of satisfaction that I got away with it. That special nylon helped preserve the memory of the event so I can fantasize and relive my crime when I desire. I was thrilled using a necktie and taking a nylon, so the authorities will most likely use that to connect my future crimes. I learned this terminology from the library research and my studies.

*Note from the Author: Forensic Science didn't start using the term 'signature' relating to serial killers until the 1970s. The term 'trophy' wasn't used until the 1990's. The term 'hunting' has been used since the 1940s.

I went back out hunting for my next prey about six months later to a seedy spot in Times Square on Eighth Avenue called the Minnesota Strip where a high volume of prostitutes roamed. On the curb, I picked up a redhead pro named Evelyn who was wearing a short, tight leather skirt, a low-neck blouse and had a strong Cockney accent. First out, I asked her where a good place was to get some privacy. I had to settle for another dark and gloomy alley that smelled of sour beer and rotten garbage which was the only option on that busy Friday night. There was an old, drunk veteran sleeping by the back door of a neighborhood bar, but I didn't let that disturb me. I offered my date a sniff of my stash because she was fun to talk to for a short while, so I thanked her for her company. While she had turned her head to flick cigarette ashes out of the car window, I strangled her monstrously and enthusiastically until her last gulp of air. She had bitten down on her tongue so damned hard; her mouth was oozing drool and blood all over her cleavage and white blouse. It was a gross sight, but it didn't affect me because I had seen much worse at the funeral home. I used another silk tie that my dad gave me for my birthday last year when he saw I liked wearing them. He had no idea why I had recently become interested in ties and I wasn't going to tell him.

I had my way with this tramp, like my first kill. I ripped a nylon off her dangling leg and gave her inner thigh a nasty bite before pushing her dead body out of the car. I was getting the knack of the pursuit and liked it.

When I wasn't cramming the books, which was a rarity, I was assisting Dad in the embalming room at home. While I was at the University, my killing sprees had long breaks between each victim, too long sometimes. My lengthy break periods mitigated the potency of my fantasies and made me extremely frustrated. My fantasies got too weak, in spite of using a nylon, so I had difficulty having an orgasm. I managed to hold it together to finish my courses using lot of discipline and determination to achieve my goal. I was told by more than one professor I was extremely bright and motivated so I would do well and have a prosperous future. My higher education was the most difficult dedication and accomplishment I have ever made. I graduated in 1943 with a bachelor's degree, so now I could fall back on my education in the future if it ever became necessary. I had thoughts about being a professor someday.

CHAPTER 7

THE CRIMINAL MIND

In 1943, at twenty-two, I wanted to live on my own. I was out of NYU and tired of living at home, though both had been mandatory. Dad passed away that year of an overdose of heroin, they said, which devastated mum and me. He had missed my graduation, and I had missed his death. I had my own belief about dad's demise. It was possible he may have committed suicide and overdosed on purpose because he knew I had been planning to move away from home at the end of that week and like me, he would be losing his best friend and partner in crime. I don't think he could bear the thought of continuing to live his double life in solitude and mum had been getting more radical with her sacred religion. Dad did not agree so it was driving him mad. Last time at home I detected he was disappearing to the basement more often even when there wasn't a corpse to embalm. The dark, quiet atmosphere down there was his escape away from mum and her hysterical behavior. He told me once she threw her Bible at his head that gave him a bloody nose because he finally shouted at her.

"Shut up about your God damned church, Liz! I'm sick and tired of hearing about your beloved religious nonsense! No one else I know talks like you do!"

It was going to be a terribly hard move for me, but I had to get away, especially now. That would leave Dad alone, alone with mum there would be more torture, because she had remained angry since that Bible throwing day. Mr. Webb Sr. would be left with only cadavers to talk to and take heroin with. Nothing more to live for. I knew Dad would be sad, miserable and lonely without me and I understood. It all made sense to me because I understood him. I was like him in many ways. I mourned deeply for Dad and always will. I know mum misses him, but they didn't have a strong connection like we did, so I was confident she was tough enough and religious enough to get through her loss alone.

I had the responsibility and most difficult task to embalm my own father. At first, I didn't know if I could handle it, but I didn't want anyone else to do it, so I kept Dad right there at the funeral home where we lived and worked, and I prepared his body with the utmost of care and respect. I confess I broke down in tears a few times during the process, but with a lot of luck I was able to finish. Mum wanted a small informal service. A few of her church friends came to pay respects and Dad was buried in the town's cemetery a few days after his funeral.

I stayed at the funeral home after Dad's funeral for two weeks so mum and I could make our separate plans. With Dad gone, we both knew we had to move out of the funeral home. We informed the proprietor of our moving plans before he had a chance to tell us to leave.

Mum decided to move in with her older, spinster sister in Boston and I chose to move to a small town outside of Portland, Maine called Bridgeport. We split up Dad's meager savings and his small life insurance policy to start our new lives apart. In ten days, we had packed up our personal belongings, a few keepsakes and were ready to go our separate ways. Saying goodbye to mum was sad for her and joyful for me. We hugged and she cried a little. I wished her the best of luck. She put her frail hand on my cheek and said, "Andrew, be a good boy. Your mother loves you. Please, keep in touch." I told her I would.

In Bridgeport, things started to look good for me. I was finally living on my own, out of home, out of school and extremely ambitious for more excitement and a new profession. I rented a small one-bedroom cottage in a trailer park and quickly picked up a job at the county morgue as pathology assistant working with the medical examiner. With my years of experience in the funeral home, working with dad and my education, I walked right into that position and got hired on the spot with a decent starting salary. Now, I was ready to embark on the next chapters of my life.

In my new dwelling, I was living alone in solitude with just my faded fantasies and criminal mind. I was working at the morgue six days and some evenings per week, then coming home to my empty apartment where my mind started over-thinking, planning, anticipating and slowly driving me to the brink of madness. There were voices in my head talking to me, sometimes telling me things to do, terrible things. I tried to ignore them. They shouted at me or whispered at me. Men's voices and women's voices solo or in unison. These disturbances have plagued me since my last year in school. I never told anyone because I didn't want anyone to think I was crazy. I didn't want to make friends or get close to another person because I couldn't relate or discuss my life, so I delved into my work at the morgue. Every day after work, I went home to deal with my demons.

After a couple of months living and working in Maine, my mind became a constant war zone. My nervousness and agitation began to get noticeable to others at work. I needed a fix. I needed to hunt. I was driven with a desire to commit murder. I was fantasizing about all sorts of ominous, dangerous and daring deeds. I was more than bored, anxious, and feeling desperately mischievous. I wanted a thrill. I started reflecting on strangling those alley cats when I was a boy and hanging them by the neck on our neighbor's clothes lines. I reminisced about my childhood years at that busy, depressing funeral parlor in New York and all the times I desired to ravish and rape a young corpse when Dad was upstairs. After catching me the first time, he purposely left the embalming room sometimes to give me some privacy with a fresh new young beauty. Just a nod or a wink before he left, saying he'd be back in an hour. That was our silent system.

But during my years at NYU, I had progressed to a higher level with more risky and illegal behavior. I graduated from cats and cadavers to live women and that was plaguing my psyche. I knew it would be soon.

At home in my apartment after working at the morgue one night, I anxiously opened my secret, locked chest, and took out the mementos of nylons I took from the ladies of the night. Those memories started rushing back of how I had enjoyed abusing and killing them. But lately, I could barely see them in my mind's eye. Like I was looking through a thick haze instead of a crisp clear picture. I tried one last time to make the nylons do their magic, but it was too late for those fantasies. I needed new ones.

Customarily, I laid the nylons out on my bed so I could look at them, feel them, smell them one by one and relive the fantasy from each slutty cadaver. Those fantasies were no longer effective, and my souveniers were no longer useful. I knew this deviant ceremony had finally arrived at a dead end. It was time, past time I had to seek other means to entertain and satisfy my decadent, sexual desires. Working at the county morgue wasn't satisfying my needs because I didn't have enough time and access to a corpse like I did during my funeral parlor days. I needed more, much more and wasn't getting it here on the job. Fantasies lost are unacceptable. I had to move quickly before I went completely bonkers!

CHAPTER 8

INFAMOUS SERIAL KILLERS

The next morning, I drove to the library to see if I could find any information about murder, rape and the law. I had a wealth of knowledge not known to most men my age, but I wanted more. I strived for more. I was ecstatic to find information about an Englishman, John Christie, who was a notorious criminal convicted of assaulting women and patronizing prostitutes in the 1930s. By chance I had found a month-old British rag laying on a table that day with some chap had forgotten. The UK tabloid also stated John had started his killing spree that same year, 1943, by using coal gas to render them unconscious before raping and strangling them. The news said, he allegedly had a strong emotional bond with his victims, some referred to necrophilia. It looked to me like this English chap had a similar MO, so I was going to keep my eyes open to any further new about Mr. Christie's crimes. For obvious reasons, I developed a sympatico for dear John. He was on his way to achieve infamous status as a rapist and murderer. I was curious if or when he'd get caught.

My life got much stranger living in Bridgeport in 1943. I couldn't have predicted my modus operandi was like the UK's notorious murderer whose killing spree had started about the time I moved to Maine. Purely coincidental. My memory also recalled my dad talking to mum about America's first serial killer called H.H. Holmes, but I was too young to make a connection at eight years old. Remembering the shocking tale dad told mum about Holmes, I thought it was time to read up on that bloke, too. I was curious to see if my mode of killing had any similarities to H.H. Holmes.

I read his name was Herman Webbster Mudgett AKA Dr. Henry Howard Holmes or H.H. Holmes. When I read the details about his Murder Castle, I couldn't believe my eyes! I gasped, took a deep breath, and reread about his infamous hotel business operation that was active between 1891-1894. Holmes was executed by hanging in May 1896 at 34 years old. I had recently turned twenty-three, so I had some living to do. I was also shocked to read about the bizarre and perverted activities Holmes had performed at his macabre hotel in downtown Chicago because I had been harboring a similar plan for a year or two in the darkest corner of my mind. Another coincidence? My research said Holmes built a labyrinthine structure with traps and chutes to kill his victims. He operated his hotel only three years before he was caught. It made me wonder if I ever got in a similar situation how long would I be lucky before I was caught and put to death. Time would tell all. I was still young.

After visiting the library my head was spinning with newfound information and bursting with enlightenment and anticipation. I had those mixed emotions but, in a calming, and reassuring way. It was good to learn I wasn't alone with my gruesome, abnormal desires. I felt more confident and freer in a strange sense. It was getting dark, so my first compelling thought was to go out hunting like I had done in New York. Now, after all I read, I figured I finally belonged to a select, evil group. I had virtually connected with others like me, though it was a bond in pure deviance I identified with. That night, I was ready to take my first drive down to Boston to visit mum and go hunting. I'd be there in less than three hours.

"I was born with the evil one standing as my sponsor beside the bed where I was ushered into the world, and he has been with me since." ~ H. H. Holmes

(To Dr. Ferdinand C. Gaucher)

CHAPTER 9

NECK-TIE STRANGLER

Arriving in Boston, I pulled off the highway and picked up The Boston Post newspaper from one of those street dispensers. I was happy I made that pit stop. On the front page in large, bold print, it read: The **'Neck-Tie Strangler' is at Large.** I was glad I could pull into a parking space and turn the engine off. I knew this article had to be about me and I was spellbound to say the least. A wave of excitement flushed over me so strongly, I became nauseated, and I started breathing heavily. My heart was pounding excessively, but with a huge inhale and exhale and hands shaking nervously, I tried to read the article out loud to myself with my voice trembling and stuttering from excitement.

It read: "The New York city police reported that two bodies of local prostitutes had been found murdered within the city limits. We are asking for tips from anyone who may have seen either of these brutal crimes. Both young women were strangled by a man's neck-tie and dumped in different alleys relatively close to each other. The first Jane Doe who was found before the holidays, had been brutally raped and strangled with a man's black necktie. The second victim was also strangled with a necktie. Both women had been severely struck in the face and each one was missing a nylon which is believed to be the killer's trophy. The mayor has named this killer 'The Neck-Tie Strangler.' No one has come forth with any evidence so far. We're not at liberty to give more information until our investigation is further along with more evidence. Law enforcement is warning women in the big city to walk in pairs or groups until the killer is apprehended."

I noticed they didn't mention the severe bite mark I left behind on a thigh, but I won't be doing that again soon. I was given a title! At last, I was somebody important now. I had a name and recognition for my work, for my accomplishments like Christie and

Holmes. Hooray. The neck-tie strangler was quite appropriate if I must say so myself and I will do my best to live up to their expectations. I folded the newspaper and stuck it under the driver's seat, then I continued on my way down to the Combat Zone to check out the action to quench my most recent, decadent desires. The newspaper story had given me a feeling much more powerful and invincible than ever before. At last, I was on my way to be famous like my colleagues in crime. It was still too light out and not busy enough to be unnoticed, so I drove out to mum's.

After a brief, almost intolerable visit with mum, I drove back to Boston's Combat Zone. If I so desired, I could easily get lucky picking up a pro in the red-light district on any trip to Boston. There were so many old buildings with dark, vacant alleys to hide in that I never had to worry about finding a place to commit my crimes. Living in Bridgeport was a reasonably short drive to my mother's new home in the Boston suburb of Swampscott, only twelve miles northeast of downtown Boston. I went there to visit her on a weekend every three or four months for the first year to make sure she was doing well, but that wasn't why I liked going to Boston. I didn't miss mum. We hadn't been close when I was growing up because of her religious beliefs, strict discipline, and verbally abusive ways. She was getting old and had health issues, so I had contemplated putting her out of her misery on one of my visits so I could inherit what she had left. On the flip side, after seeing mum, I had changed my mind because I saw the Grim Reaper would take her soon enough. The sooner the better.

In Boston, I embarked on the same routine I had started in southern Maine. My MO was a quick, hard, backhand punch in the face to surprise and stun my victim enough so I could strangle them with my bare hands at first. I liked using my hands because I could revel in the power and intimacy of feeling the life drain out of my victims, hearing them gasp and gulp for air until saliva foamed between their lips. I preferred to finish the job with a necktie and leave it wrapped around my victim's neck. After the she became unconscious from my strangling methods, I took a large hunting knife with a wide, jagged, seven-inch blade out from under my seat, went around to the passenger side, opened the door and pulled her out onto the pavement where I raped her and sliced her throat so deeply that I left her gurgling in a big pool of her own plasma. I used the knife just for some extra fun. I can't stand to get bored. Now, I had killed only one skank in Boston so far.

I figured that murder would hit the Boston Herald and soon the news about the Neck-Tie Strangler would hit all the New England states and I was right, it did that same weekend. The front page of the Boston Herald and Portland paper said The Neck-Tie Stranger had moved from NYC to the Boston area. The murder with neckties must have moved to Boston, Massachusetts. A high alert was put in all the newspapers up to Portland, Maine. I utterly treasured reading in the Boston Herald and Portland Press Herald from then on about the deviant Neck-Tie Strangler during the first year I lived in Bridgeport. New York to Maine was vulnerable and buzzing about a young monster murderer who had been active in NYC since 1941 and had moved to New England to continue his killing spree.

I held off for about a year after my first victim in Boston hoping the sensationalizing would calm down and it did. I worked diligently at the county morgue and depended on my newest trophy for that period. After a year of deprivation, I continued my killing spree but kept my self-discipline in order.

First time after the uneventful year, I hired a prostitute to meet at a sleazy bar next to a seedy motel with the same reputation. It looked like it might have been a drug den, too, so it was unsafe for me there. I was bound to try something different, but there was a higher risk here for cops to show up. I called an agency to request their youngest, prettiest blonde with blue or green eyes. The madam said I would be pleased with her new girl Sheri because she looked to be about sixteen. She sounded like the perfect date for me.

Sheri showed up on time. When she walked into the beer smelling bar wearing a sexy black blouse and skirt, she looked similarly to what I had envisioned but there was a flaw that stood out to me. Her eyes were brown. I only liked blue or green eyes, like Jackie had. We chatted over a couple of strong Manhattans, and my fantasy got stronger by the minute. I visualized this Sheri girl lying dead on an embalming table with her legs spread apart. While she flirted with me, I couldn't get that picture out of my mind. She was very appealing and like her madam boss said, she looked no older than sixteen, maybe younger. In an hour to be precise, I politely escorted Sheri back into my shabby motel room which was near the back entrance of the 'no-tell' motel.

From the moment I was alone with the twit, before we sat down on the bed, she made sexual advances to me. She started smooching my neck and rubbing my loins and tried to kiss me, but I turned my face away from her puckered lips so she couldn't make mouth contact. That disgusted me. I was curious how far this brown-eyed skank would go before I avenged her. She aggressively unzipped my trousers, moaning and sweet talking to me; she put her hand inside my trousers and attempted to stroke me slowly, but nothing happened, of course. I could not respond. Her advances didn't turn me on in the slightest, so I became angry and embarrassed, by what she said.

"Hey doll, what's the matter with you tonight? Doesn't your little one like Sheri? Or maybe you're a Poof? A faggot? Should I call you Mary, doll?"

When that 'slut' asked if I was a homo, I lost my temper in a rage I had never felt before. I gave her a swift hard backhand across her face, so rough she fell backwards onto the bed on her back. She cried out and grabbed her sore bleeding lips.

"Dammit, you're crazy, dude! Keep your money, I'm getting outta here!"

Saying that, Sheri jumped up off the bed in fury, and I totally lost it again. I couldn't control my violent impulses. I gave her a swift Karate chop to the left side of her neck that sent her sailing backwards down on the bed. I finally spoke my peace.

"Listen here you piece of white trash; you should have never called me a faggot!" I pulled a new necktie out of my back pocket and jumped on top of her, straddling her narrow hips tightly with my knees and simultaneously grabbed her neck with both of my strong hands. I dominantly squeezed her scrawny little neck with all my might and then finished her off by choking her savagely with a red tie. Her eyes bulged, her tongue stuck out, foaming, and slobbering all over herself and all over my hands as life drained out of her defenseless body. What a sickening sight, seeing her laying there grunting her last sounds of the death rattle. Yes, she was dead, stone dead and fortunately looking a lot like Jackie, the pretty blonde teenager that came into the funeral home my dad was working at in New York, except for her brown eyes,.

I closed her freaky wild, dark eyes, so she'd look more like Jackie. I started calling her Jackie and the evening began to get better. I moved backwards just enough to push the hot cadaver's tight, black skirt up to her belly and that's all it took to get me aroused. Like many times before in the embalming room of the funeral home, I spread eagle this cadaver's legs to expose her warm, but hairy, inviting cavern. I realized all over again at twenty-four that I was extremely different from all men. I wasn't a faggot, nor excited by live females, only dead ones. I put Sheri's corpse under the mattress and left the motel immediately after my dirty deed.

I was convinced I was a necrophiliac like my dad which I had also looked up at the library. I wouldn't be aware for many years, how much I was following in the deadly footsteps of the English serial killer, John Christie who was also a necrophiliac. By no means I was a copycat killer. If my evil murders looked like the criminal actions of other killers, it was purely coincidental, because I didn't want to be like any of the others. I wanted my own exclusive identity.

CHAPTER 10

DOUBLE LIFE OF CRIME

Is the months rolled by working at the county morgue, my work became more desirable. Rarely, we received a young, blonde teenager, but a blonde in her early twenties, looking much younger was also appealing. I assisted with most of the autopsies and was rarely left alone to my own vices. I worked the graveyard shift so I would have more opportunities to have my way with a desired female corpse should one arrive unexpectedly. But the kind of corpse I desired was extremely rare.

After two years at this job, I got extremely comfortable and still felt invincible, thinking I wouldn't get caught in action in the morgue and I didn't. When business was slow, when fantasies were failing, I got in the habit of hunting in a nearby town instead of driving to Boston. I stopped in Salem, Mass. Driving home from Boston the last time out of pure curiosity. In Salem, I didn't desire a street slag, I was there to see the sights where the witches were supposed to be. It was a cool town. It was dark and creepy to other visitors, but I fit in.

Before leaving New York, I had bought an old, 1931 Ford Town Sedan from a mortician that was friends with the owner of the funeral parlor we lived in. His vehicle was twelve years old but had been well kept. Mr. Brown said his car was the most desired Model A, so it would hold its value. He had been nice enough to let me pay $100 down and make payments of $50 per month for four months while I was commuting to the university. I loved the car because it had a long, roomy seat in the front and back. I covered both long, cloth seats with a plastic covering so they wouldn't get soiled with foul-smelling fluids and blood from my devilish escapades. Plastic is easy to wipe clean.

I had decided it would be too risky to hire a call girl again from the same agency near where I lived in Bridgeport and go to a motel room. My first experience doing that made me too uncomfortable because it was too risky. Alternatively, when the desire hit me, I picked up a slag from the poor side of a nearby town. I was able to restrain myself from making too many hunting trips near my hometown because my newest souvenirs were potent enough for several months. I didn't want the Necktie Strangler to get caught. NYC and Boston law enforcement agencies were in cahoots with local authorities near me, so I had to lay low. I was bound to keep a low profile until I felt the necessity to move again became unbearable.

If and when I chose to go, over the next seven years, I had no problem finding a tail willing to get into my car. I would insist on driving a few miles out of town, on a different country road each time to park behind a closed restaurant, closed gas station or lakeside if no one was around. I parked and let the shag get close enough to start pawing me, then I swiftly, backhanded her in the face with my fist to stun her, then proceeded to strangle her to death using my hands before my tie. After she croaked, peed or defecated on my car seat, I pulled her body by the ankles as far into the nearby brush or woods I could go. The convenience of the woods was a plus the cities didn't offer.

I added something extra to my crime scenes. I always placed each corpse on their back with legs spread wide open, arms by their sides and now, a plastic, artificial rose in her mouth. I knew how to confuse law enforcement because they expect a killer's MO is always the same. I still used neckties on occasion, but a fake flower in the mouth suggested a different MO. I also had to revert to different keepsakes at times when the corpses weren't wearing nylons. No problem for me. I preferred a nylon but panties or a bra had to suffice if they weren't wearing nylons. I always left the corpse at the crime scene like the first call girl I killed in a sleazy motel room and stuffed her body under the dilapidated, stained mattress. I wondered how long it would take before the maid or manager started smelling the distinct and horrid smell of death.

During the last ten years, while I lived and worked near Portland, Maine. After hearing about my fellow Englishman, the UK's John Christie, I often thought about him and wondered if he had heard about the Neck-Tie Strangler in America. I had been operating at the same time as Chritie's spree from 1943 – 1953. I must have sexually raped about the same number of cadavers at the hospital morgue. For killing his wife, Christie was executed by hanging in prison in London in 1953. He was 54 years old. I fled Bridgeport in 1953. I was thirty-two years old.

I had gained lots of experience and more confidence during those active years in Southern Maine despite the few close calls with the Rozzers. I managed to flee the scene and disappear in the nick of time. I had been lucky so far, and my double life had been successful since I was twelve. I often wondered if my fate would be like Holmes or Christie who were both hanged. Because of their notoriety, I would feel honored to be hanged, that is, IF they catch me.

CHAPTER 11

INNKEEPER VS. UNDERTAKER

Everything, even the best of times gets old after a while. The last two decades of my life were divided into two, ten-year periods. Having been exposed to the detailed operation of a funeral home in New York from 1933 to 1943, then ten years at the county morgue near Portland from 1943 to 1953, I was ready for another big change. Bored again and always working for someone wasn't good enough anymore. Working at the morgue, I saved up a considerable amount of money because I didn't go anywhere except to work, and the adventures of my sexual desires didn't cost anything but gasoline. I was sitting pretty or as some blokes might call it, well-heeled for my thirty-two years.

I started looking daily at ads in the Portland Press for business opportunities or hotels for sale in Maine, further up the coast, not near a big city, but in a tourist attraction area. I got that idea from reading about H.H. Holmes. Within a week, I came across an ad for a recently abandoned funeral home for sale in Briggstown, Maine. I couldn't believe my eyes. I blinked twice, opened my tired eyes again and there it was staring at me in the face. Of all the great ideas, this had to be one of the best. I called the realtor immediately, talked to an old man called Mr. Price and told him to hold that property because I would get a train out of Portland the following morning. Bright and early on a brisk, autumn Friday morning, I hopped into a passenger car and rode on the Bangor & Aroostook Railroad up to Bangor, Maine. From Bangor, I jumped on a bus to go to Briggstown. On the train and bus ride, I instantaneously came up with a feasible plan to put it in motion, something the realtor would believe. Mr. Price had told me on the phone the funeral home was an old, Victorian, Queen Anne-style mansion, the best looking one in town, even under the circumstances of what it was. I was so enthusiastic to see it, because I had also had an incredible 'brainstorm'.

Holmes did his dirty deeds in a hotel, Christie did his elsewhere, and I could open a guest house in Briggstown for travelers, tourists and transient workers. I thought that was a brilliant idea. If I liked the location of the property, I would purchase the old funeral home and become an innkeeper. That sounded good. Innkeeper. I would be a proud, dignified innkeeper and Mr. Price would probably like my plan. I could leave my sordid, evil past in New York, Boston and Southern Maine and become the quaint town's first debonaire innkeeper of a classy Victorian guest house.

I arrived in Briggstown early evening, just before dusk, just in time to catch the realtor, Lenny Price, locking up the office to go home for the night. Mr. Price thought I wasn't going to make it, but he was pleased that I kept my word.

We spoke briefly in front of his office where he told me that the elderly mortician had died during the bleak holidays and his will instructed the immediate sale of the property. Mr. Price drove me directly over to the charming funeral home which was only five minutes away. Driving there he asked me if I was interested in opening up another funeral home. As we pulled up into the driveway of the glorious mansion, this is how our conversation went, verbatim. I politely answered,

"No, no I'm not. I'm not a mortician, but there is something, something alluring about this elegant, Victorian architecture that fascinates me. I believe this home would make the perfect guest house in this area. Are there any others in Briggstown or nearby? Does your season bring a lot of tourists to this area?"

"Why yes, young fellow, there are a few motels and a couple of guest houses along this road, but none of them look anything like this unusual Queen Anne gem. I mean, well you know what I mean. Folks here have only known this particular property to be a funeral home. Oh, and yes, to your other question. There are lots of tourists that find their way to Briggstown from Bar Harbor and from the other towns on Mt. Desert Island, plus, there's a good share of transients who come up here just to work for the summer, earning money for college, then they all go back home wherever that is.

Andrew, the house is being sold 'as is', so the basement is still full of mortuary equipment, unfortunately, because it would be a chore and an expense to have it all removed. It's got a cremation chamber, you know, the oven, embalming tables, coolers, tools and God knows what else. Why does a young, good-looking fellow like you want to buy that house of death? Guess you're not afraid of ghosts either, huh? There are other mansions and nice homes up in Bangor that don't have creepy stigma or gross stuff you'd have to get rid of. Would you like to look at some other handsome properties I can show you tomorrow?"

I stood quietly and patiently, pondering, and puffing slowly and methodically on my first Arturo Fuente cigar, not being moved at all by Mr. Price's suggestion of looking at other options. My mind was made up before I arrived in Briggstown. After tapping once lightly on my stogie, I addressed the strange and somewhat awkward situation. I liked Mr. Price even though he was getting pushy.

"Mr. Price, I thank you sincerely for your consideration, but I'm not the slightest bit bothered by the history of this handsome old home, nor does the morbid basement décor disturb me. I assure you; my seasonal guests will not have access to the basement. I'm also fond of the beautiful park across the street."

I didn't mention to Mr. Price the reason I favored the park. Like Marcel Proust, I saw several young boys playing there when I arrived at the mansion and one of them caught my eye. I've been curious about a young boy since I read 'Remembrance of Things Past' in my literature class.

"I like this property Mr. Price, and I would like to have a tour in the morning if you don't mind. I would also like to purchase the lot on the south side."

"Oh, yes, yes of course sir, in the morning. In the morning I'd be delighted to meet you here, say about 9:00 A.M.? The electricity was shut off, but there is enough light coming in those handsome tall windows in the morning, so you'll be able to see everything alright, except for the basement, it's dark down there and very disturbing if you're not used to it. Personally, I'd be happy not to have to go down there again, but it's part of the job. I'll bring a couple of flashlights for the basement."

Mr. Price gave a deep sigh of relief, rolled his eyes and made a weird expression. I could see he was going to be uncomfortable showing this place, especially the basement, but I was extremely familiar with a funeral home, so it wouldn't phase me, in fact I'm going to like it. Price went on to explain,

"You see, Andrew, you are only the second client that has requested to see this property. My first client didn't get halfway down the basement stairs, turned around and scurried back up those stairs as fast as her feet would take her. She promptly thanked me for my trouble, then flew out the door. I never heard from her again. I think she saw the embalming table and furnace door and got spooked. You, my dear boy, are a brave soul, but then again you know what you're doing. My wife didn't want to see the inside of this house because of its former business. She's also superstitious and thinks there must be ghosts stirring around in there. I forgot to mention on the phone son, that Mr. Sneed, the deceased owner of this place wanted his 1939 Packard Henney hearse to be sold with his house, but if you don't want it, I could give it to a car dealer I know here in town and he could…"

"That won't be necessary, Mr. Price. I rather like those old, tough hearses. They're a fantastic substitution for a truck and they're built like Sherman tanks. I could even wear my top hat in that beast. I'll keep it parked in the garage behind the house, and no one will be the wiser unless I take it out on Halloween night and drive slowly through the neighborhood." I chuckled under my breath.

"Bartholomew Sneed told me several times that vehicle was his favorite."

"I can see why. She's a stately girl. They'll forget about it in time. But if I decide to drive it occasionally, they'll think I'm eccentric and I suppose you could say I am, or I wouldn't be buying this funeral home."

I grunted with a smirk. Mr. Price couldn't have imagined to whom he was selling this property and hearse. My secret.

"Andrew, just to let you know, Mr. Sneed had a hard time finding hired help to clean the interior's three floors, forget the basement. I didn't realize there were so many superstitious people until I listed this one. Men and women alike are afraid of death it seems, or maybe it's the embalming facility with the oven and all that scares them. It is disturbing to those who aren't accustomed to it. I'm sure morticians are totally desensitized by all of it, I mean they'd have to be to do their gross job, wouldn't you think, Andrew? Also, um, ah, I forgot to mention, on the first floor there is a reparation room, a reposing room, a reception room, a chapel and towards the back of this house, there is a room Mr. Sneed called the display area. That room still has a couple of caskets, and other funeral merchandise that he showcased for customers. You might want to have an auction company come pick all that stuff up and get it out of there."

"I'm not going to worry about all that right now. But yes, you are most likely correct in your observation and analysis, Mr. Price. I never thought of it that way. When I was a small boy growing up in New York, my father worked for a funeral home, so I was exposed to it at a young age. It didn't bother me then, so it won't upset me now. As far as getting someone to clean, I don't think that will be a problem. Let's call it a night and we'll close a deal in the morning. I'll make you and offer on this home and the hearse tomorrow."

I hitched a ride with Mr. Price to the closest motel. I daydreamed and fantasized all night about owning that beautiful mansion and how lucky I was to have stumbled upon such a perfect situation for my deviant, fiendish desires.

CHAPTER 12

SINISTER TALES OF LOVE & DEATH

The Next morning at 9:00 AM, Mr. Price picked me up the modest motel and we went over to the abandoned funeral home. Once again, we sat in the car to chat before I got the royal tour. I found out the mansion was built in 1898 and Mr. Sneed had bought it in 1921, the year I was born. That year he turned it into a funeral parlor. Mr. Price told me Sneed had graduated from Worsham College of Mortuary Science in Wheeling, Illinois and moved to Maine to settle down and get into the funeral business. Shortly after purchasing the mansion, Sneed became ill with appendicitis and was rushed to the Eastern Maine Medical Center in Bangor, Maine. There he met Pauline Pratt, a charming and formidable spinster, thirty years' old who was a registered nurse in his care.

Pauline and Bartholomew fell in love, had a brief courtship and were married in lovely, downtown Bar Harbor the same year. Now, I'm going to tell you a rumor that goes with this funeral home. Naturally, there would have to be a menacing story or two attached to a house of death, don't you think, Andrew?"

I sat motionless and unresponsive for a few seconds wondering what I was about to hear from Price. Then, abruptly, I answered.

You're absolutely right, again, Mr. Price. What would a funeral home be without sinister tales about it? Price eagerly continued.

"Here's the worst of it. Sneed had been the only mortician in Briggstown since it opened for business in 1921. He took ill last winter from pneumonia complications, well into his seventies and was ready to retire when he passed away. His wife, after thirty years of marriage had passed away from a stroke a year before and there was a rumor around town that no one had seen or heard of a funeral for Pauline. So, rumors spread around town like wildfire that he must have been driving about doing his errands with a casket in the back of his hearse with Pauline's decomposing corpse. Price went downhill rapidly after her death. He loved her so dearly he couldn't bear to lose her or give her up.

The towns' people said he started to act strangely. Mr. Price said he thought the old, sickly mortician went into a deep depression and went mad. He was seen a few times walking outside in the rain or snow in the nude to pick up his mail by the street or to retrieve the newspaper that was flung into his yard. Everyone assumed his wife was in the casket, though they never knew for sure. After a week, someone noticed the casket was no longer in the hearse. The little town of Briggstown, would forever be plagued with those haunting rumors. Are you ready for the worst of it, my boy?"

Price went on to tell me more of the gritty story. I could see he was having fun trying to spook me, but I didn't care. I urged him on. He said Mr. Sneed's young ambitious assistant, Henry McCain, told Mel, the fat and homely bartender at the Long Drink, that he witnessed Sneed putting his dead wife's corpse in the morgue freezer. Henry said it was freaky to see Pauline laying in there with her eyes wide open, a smile pulled on her face and dressed in her thirty-year-old wedding gown that didn't fit. He said his boss made him help to embalm Pauline and cut her wedding dress enough to fit partially around her plump body. He said Sneed told him to put makeup on her and fix her hair as his usual work on corpses, but to fix her eyes so they'd stay open instead of closed and put a permanent smile on her face showing some teeth which was extra distorted. Henry was obliged to do his boss's bidding but quit immediately after fixing Pauline to Sneed's odd specifications.

Everything Henry witnessed and was told to do took a major toll on his psyche. Henry told Mel, the bartender at the Long Drink bar, he could handle everything else he saw and did at the funeral home before Pauline, but knowing Sneed's wife was a frozen stiff in the freezer for days before he applied makeup on her, but that wasn't all of it. Henry said she looked like the bride of Frankenstein bulging out of a 1920's yellowed, tattered and torn wedding gown with a bouquet of dead, black, wilted roses in her hands that were handcuffed together. Mel also told me; Henry said the situation became too disturbing for him to deal with. Pauline's creepy display in the freezer grave upset him to the point of having horrific nightmares. Henry had also found a fraternity paddle with 'Pauline's Rewards' engraved on it, a leather riding crop and a photo of her husband dressed in women's clothing and blonde wig laying tucked under her sightly gown by her feet. That was this town's secret.

"How does this story grab you, Andrew? Mel told me it was all true, Henry was never the same after he left his job at the Blue Pine Funeral Services. He went into the Long Drink daily to get drunk until his money ran out. Rumor had it that poor Henry, with only twenty-nine years, ended up in the Maine insane asylum in Bangor that looked like a scary, brick prison. His ailing mother couldn't afford the luxury of a private mental hospital. Henry's mother told Mr. Sneed that her son was being given barbaric, Electroshock treatments which caused him to have convulsive, grand mall seizures, and she feared he'd never get out of there. Mr. Sneed was anything but sympathetic to Henry's grieving mother. He had his own grief and guilt to deal with.

Finally, Sneed cremated Pauline and drove everywhere with her urn sitting next to him on the front seat. What was more puzzling was the peculiar black urn. Occasionally, Sneed took his wife's ashes into that neighborhood pub, sat it on the bar in front of him and drank until he shouldn't drive. No one ever volunteered to drive the insane, intoxicated mortician home in his hearse. The townspeople feared Sneed and his hearse and thought they'd be cursed with bad luck to get inside it. Most folks here are still superstitious and afraid of that black hearse. Briggstown's only physician told Mel, the old man must have caught the flu going outside in the nude the last time which turned to pneumonia."

I asked Price where Sneed's wife's urn ended up. He said, he remembered her urn was put in his casket and buried with him at Heaven's Hill Cemetery. I was amused by that whole story whether it was true or fiction. I could tell Price was uneasy telling me about it, but I could tell he wanted to get it off his chest, possibly to clear the air if I heard any strange rumors in town or at the Long Drink.

After the tell-all, Price took me for a walk around the house, for a peek inside the pretentious, black hearse and cluttered garage. It was time to tour the mansion inside. The old hearse still bore the name of its business, Blue Pine Funeral Services. I liked the Blue Pine part, but I had to change Funeral Services to Guests Inn.

I was delighted to see the macabre-like style of décor, but I would have to give it a token facelift on the first floor so not to scare future guests away. After all, it was going to be presented as an upscale Victorian mansion. The basement in this mansion, was fully equipped with a crematory furnace, a cremation processor machine, and a grinder or cremulator to pulverize all bones fragments. It had an embalming table, a mortuary freezer for storing only one or two bodies, but that would suffice, an array of embalming tools and a cadaver cart. Naturally, I knew the entire operation, so I knew this room wasn't missing much and secretly, I brought a few instruments of my own. I wasn't planning on using all the equipment for the same reasons Mr. Sneed did and I was not going to tell Mr. Price anything about my intentions. I had my own use for the basement, but in the meantime, I would have a lot of work to do to get this old home perfect for my needs. I would need lots of time and money to get it right. Here, I'd be the Innkeeper and host, with my secret fascination of dead bodies and killers. I had a limited textbook knowledge of surgical skills which I studied on my own in the library after graduating from NYU.

Mr. Price took his time to give me a thorough tour of all three floors, closets, cabinets and the remaining kitchen appliances that were in good order. During my tour, he shared more peculiarities about the building I was about to purchase. Price went on to describe the strange type of service Sneed offered as an alternative to the traditional funeral services. He carried on.

"Young man, what I'm about to tell you may be as weird to you as it was to the rest of us here in Briggstown when the word got out. Sneed was obviously a piece of work to provide such services but a few families over the years chose it. Sneed gave the rare options of a Victorian-style funeral where the deceased was not laid out in a coffin. Instead, depending on what the corpse's interests were while living, he or she was posed accordingly. I distinctly remember a few of them because I've lived in this town all my life.

There was an elderly, well-known, high society lady who passed away in the 1930's, I forgot her name, but her surviving sister requested she'd be posed in an elaborate, gold-leafed chair sitting at a small wrought iron tea table that was set up with a lace table cloth, dainty China cups and saucers, a sterling candelabra with pink candles, sterling silver flatware, a sterling silver tea pot and a fine crystal water goblet. I'm told this deceased, sophisticated, white-haired lady was wearing a stunning, gold silk, lounge outfit with matching slippers, white, wrist length gloves and holding a long white, diamond studded cigarette holder in her right hand, just above the table as if she was going to put it to her lips. Her eyes were open, probably glass eyes, and her lips were sealed with a slight smirk, wearing pink lipstick. They said it appeared whoever did her face, pulled back her checks too far on one side so it looked unnatural, not like a normal smile. I remember they said Mozart was playing in the background. If I'm not boring you, I can recall another one of Sneed's controversial funerals."

No, not at all Mr. Price, I find your stories fascinating. Please go on, thank you. I knew about Victorian funerals, but I didn't want to spoil his story telling.

"Well, yes Mr. Webb. There was a middle-aged gentleman who passed away, I think it was also in the 1930's, who was a devout baseball fan. He admired Babe Ruth so much that he had the habit of wearing a baseball outfit when the Super Bowl was in session and sometimes he went down to the Long Drink where he'd strike up conversations with the bartender or anyone else that would listen. He'd rave about the Boston Red Socks and New York Yankees, his favorite teams, because Babe played on both Major Leagues. His wife, Lucille, I didn't forget her name, expected a handsome insurance pay out, so she went all out on his funeral. Her request was to have Dennis, yes, Dennis was his name by golly. She wanted Dennis to be standing on a diamond home plate dressed in his entire baseball outfit from hat to socks and shoes with one hand leaning on a bat. The music in the background before the service was a recording of 'Take Me Out to the Ball Game'. Naturally, her mourning guests were served grilled hot dogs, popcorn, and bottles of cold Pabst Blue Ribbon beer. There were a few more, but I'll tell you another time so we can get down to business today."

I was 32, it was April in 1953, and I had a lot of work to do if I wanted to be ready before the tourist season that started in late May or June. At the end of my glorious tour, the formidable realtor took me back to his office where we promptly negotiated and sealed the deal without a fuss. I bargained for a great deal and got it because Mr. Price was as anxious to sell as I was to buy. I was confident this place was meant to be mine. We finished our business at his bank and then stopped at the Long Drink to celebrate. Mr. Price told Mel he had just made a sale of the infamous, Blue Pine funeral home, which was a big burden off his back. Mel perked up volunteering another freaky funeral story he remembered about the death house, but my concentration was on the reality I had just purchased a Victorian funeral home and a grand old hearse, but Mel insisted to tell us another gory tale.

"This story will chill you to the bone, fellas. In 1940, a young father, Gary and his four-year-old son, Gary Jr., were killed in a car accident in their new Buick Roadmaster. It was a gem of a car with maroon paint and got a lot of attention from our townsfolk. It was reported that the road was slippery from rain and fallen leaves and their car skidded through a broken guard rail and went over a steep cliff down the side of Cadillac Mountain on the big island. Light traffic that day but for some reason, the driver lost control of his vehicle, maybe going too fast around a dangerous curve, so the big Buick plummeted down the mountain side into a granite embankment. Some folks surmised the driver may have become distracted by his son acting out and took his eyes off the road for a few seconds. Both of their bodies were extremely banged up, broken bones and their faces disfigured, so the accident was a horrific sight for the police and medical team. The child was thrown through the windshield like a torpedo and landed headfirst, so hard onto a granite precipice that it smashed his head like a pumpkin and his other body parts were strewn all over the hillside. To make the tale more gory, Gary, Sr.'s body was found mangled and bloody sitting straight up next to his son with his detached hand on the boy's crushed, flat head. Gary's face was contorted beyond recognition. That horrible accident made big headlines in every newspaper in Maine and the other New England states.

The man's mother was deceased, so his grandmother was in charge. She decided to have a unique funeral for her only grandson and great grandson. Sneed told me it was an expensive funeral because there was so much recreation. Her mourning was so dramatic, well, let me tell you what the service was first. Grandma Greenfield, matriarch of the family had a lot of money from her dead husband's estate and insurance policy. I knew Philip Greenfield. He came in here on occasion to drink and brag about what his ole lady would get if he croaked. Anyway, Grandma wanted an elaborate funeral. She was told her grandson and great grandson would need expensive, extensive, restorative art on their faces if she wanted open caskets and they couldn't promise perfection because of the amount of damage. Grandma and Gary's brother agreed to go all out for the last tribute to their loved ones, so they could remember them as they always looked. Sneed's cosmetic professional asked for recent photos of the deceased. The process was going to be more than a difficult job. He had to recreate the child's face with wax.

Grandma Greenfield was an eccentric, bossy, old geezer, but a rich one with money to burn after Philip passed away, I was told. She was in constant contact with the Blue Pine, making sure everything was done with her approval. She gave Sneed a document designating what she wanted in minute detail. After all the restorative facial art was finished and body parts sewn back on the cadavers, Grandma gave the Blue Pine thorough directions for the viewing. She gave Sneed a formal suit for her grandson, and the great grandson his favorite Teddy Bear. Her instructions entailed having Gary sit proudly in a chair, with his son Gary sitting on his lap. She wanted one of Gary's arms around his son and his other hand holding Gary's hand. The stuffed animal was to be put on the child's lap.

The Blue Pine did the best possible job they could, but something went very wrong. They ran out of wax before the job was done on the boy's face, and it would take two weeks to order more of the same. Consequently, only a children's Halloween mask could be found which had to be put on Gary's son. Because of the funeral home's shortcomings, Blue Pine thought it would be better to go along with a Halloween theme. So, reluctantly, without Grandma Greenfield's approval, the Blue Pine took it upon themselves to change the theme knowing all hell would break loose when the family saw what they did. But they had no choice.

Sneed took his only black casket, turned it up on its end opened and put Gary standing up inside the eerie coffin facing out. He put Gary, Jr. standing up between his father's legs. The Teddy Bear was put in one child's hand, and the father was holding the child's other hand at his side. Mr. Sneed got his wife's Halloween decorations out of the garage and Pauline helped him decorate the reception room. Talk about a creepy and frightening scene, it was the talk of the town for years.

When Grandma and Gary's brother Alan arrived at 5:00 PM for the night viewing, you could hear screaming and yelling in the next town. The grieving duo went berserk. Grandma Greenfield knocked the raven off the top of the casket while Alan tore all the black webbing with fake spiders and cobwebs down and threw them at Mr. Sneed. What happened next was more horrific. Grandma picked up little Gary and took his stiff body over to the davenport. She stood him on the floor in front of her, crying hysterically and tore the Halloween hood with the mask off his face. Holy crap, they said Grandma screamed out so loud and passed out, dropping her grandson's stiff corpse to the floor. Alan was trying to hug his cold dead brother at the same time but turned around when he heard Grandma scream and saw his nephew laying on the carpet with his disfigured, half wax face and stitched up neck exposed for all to see. Sneed's wife Pauline ran over to pick up the dead child, saw his horrific face, slipped and fell on top of him. They said the room was a terrifying sight. The few guests that had arrived early couldn't run out of the Blue Pine fast enough. The results were embarrassing and awkward to everyone involved. Mr. Sneed revived Grandma with smelling salts, then carried the boy into the preparation room. The event was so traumatizing to Gary's family that Sneed dropped the expenses and provided nice caskets for Gary and Gary, Jr. That terrifying tale calls for another round of drinks on me."

A few minutes after Mel's wacky tale, Mr. Price kindly drove me to the Blue Pine and said he was glad someone was interested enough to buy it so soon. I chuckled to myself, and I thanked him for everything. I had two sets of keys and paperwork in my briefcase, and I was ready to embark on the future chapters of my life. I figured the Blue Pine would keep its infamous reputation.

CHAPTER 13

DESIGNING A 'HOUSE OF HORRORS'

I was excited to start remodeling and planning my new business. My choice of décor on the first floor would be restored into my preferrable design of European influence to compliment the Victorian structure's exterior. I had studied up on H.H. Holmes when I lived near Portland, and I was willing to see if I could measure up to some of his novel décor on the upper floors but using a different business model on a smaller scale. I was in no financial position to erect a huge hotel with 100 rooms for guests, but this unique home would work well enough for me with its 14 bedrooms, saving 2 rooms for guests and my private quarters would be the double room suite with a view of the front yard and entrance. I began making a plan, taking notes, and writing down my envisioned inventions in this journal.

That weekend I decided to stay at the same dingy motel because the Long Drink was across the street for my convenience. The Blue Pine's tales were roaming around in my head and around the quaint town once again. I didn't lose any sleep over it, but waiting until Monday for the electricity, water, etc. to be put in my name was worrisome. Mr. Price had the lawn mowed in my absence for a thank you. I kept myself busy from morning 'til nightfall drawing and making tentative plans for ten mystery rooms on the second floor.

When I finished my drawings, I took a sprint across the street to the nearby, neighborhood bar in hopes to find a handyman or two that I could put to work the following week. My first time back there, Mel introduced me to an electrician and a plumber that hung out after work from local job sites. Mel also pointed out a reputable carpenter who was a regular at the Long Drink on Friday nights. I was damned lucky that night.

My intentions were to redesign the interior of the Blue Pine to create a relaxed, posh ambiance and front desk on the first floor where my select, unsuspecting guests would feel safe and comfortable when welcomed to the Blue Pine. My provisions for upstairs would be entirely altered to achieve my goals. I would customize each bedroom independently, on the 2nd floor to host a variety of my innovations. The carpenter I hire will be told to build a different construction in each of the ten rooms by using my rough sketch blueprints. There will be torture chambers, stairways to nowhere, and a secret elevator which would be the most expensive and most complex project of all. There were several other threatening inventions I had drawn. I will take pride in all of the mansion's décor, especially what I do to redecorate the tearoom lounge, parlor and front desk entrance.

MANSION'S - 1ST FLOOR FAÇADE & DÉCOR

Directly inside the front door is a Victorian period check-in desk. To the right of the desk is a small, but sufficient, alcove shape room with bay windows that will make a token gift shop. Eventually, I shall make extra income by selling a collection of souvenirs, and maybe Victorian death photos I will photograph myself. My guests will never suspect these novel gifts will echo the Blue Pine's agenda. When time permits, I will have a fun with this new proposed hobby.

Joe, my friendly carpenter has been getting a wild kick out of my mysterious and peculiar sketches. He has asked what they will be used for. I tell him it's just a strange hobby of mine to design unusual models. My explanation appeases him, but I wonder if he questions what's really going on, but he's quiet and concentrates on his work which are both most important to me.

A few steps to the left of the desk in the entrance there's a larger room with a fireplace and petite bar. I will make that the formal reception room and call it the Tea Room. The reception parlor tearoom and front desk area will have a seductive charm. I chose burgundy, cream and rose pink for the color scheme. I had the remaining Victorian davenport and two high back chairs reupholstered in a plush, burgundy, velvet material and custom-made floor-length velvet drapes with cream shears. I kept the burgundy wallpaper. It fit in with my scheme. Pink and cream-colored, satin throw pillows were arranged on the davenport and chairs. I had Andy paint all the woodwork and wall trim the luscious, cream color. I laid Oriental rugs on the gorgeous, well maintained, wood floor. There were three vintage, gas wall sconces I had converted to electricity for safety purposes, and I bought a free-standing tiffany lamp, a tiffany ceiling light, a small chandelier and a few other classic accessories at a local White Elephant antique barn. A small, electric refrigerator was left behind the front desk. I stocked that with fine wines and champagne. I fell in love with compact, walnut, Parisian bar. I enhanced the bare shelf behind the bar with a set of etched, crystal wine glasses and old-fashioned glasses for those popular drinks. The shelves under the bar were stocked with a fifth of Hiram Walker, an Old Bourbon Whiskey and Johnnie Walker Black Label, a traditional, Old Scotch Whiskey. But that wasn't enough. The final, necessary effects were to inspire a seductive experience. I purchased a small, state-of-the-art stereo cabinet at Sears & Roebuck in Bangor so I could play soft, classical music to calm the traveler's nerves and relax my female guests. I was happy to see a fully bloomed white gardenia bush on each side of the Gothic pillars in the front yard entrance and a large, pink, rose bush on the side yard. I intended to use those beautiful flowers in a vase for their fragrance to give a soothing, floral sent to the parlor and Tea Room.

A handsome, six-foot grandfather clock was standing stately, ticking subtly beside the front desk. That stayed. The classic, brass cash register on the front desk stayed, too. I took down the scenery paintings behind the mahogany desk and put-up an antique framed copy of the precious young 'Blue Boy', by Thomas Gainsborough and an oil painting copy of a pretty, young teenage, Victorian lady in a burgundy, velvet dress and hat. I found both pieces of art, reasonably priced at another nearby White Elephant. I brought with me a lithographic copy of the 19th Century English Hunting titled 'The Bury Hunt' that will be framed for the empty parlor wall. Hanging over the bar will be my personal copy of an 1840 oil by Josef Danhauser called 'Liszt at the Piano.' My bedroom suite will be decorated with framed prints of horrifying, torture methods used on women during the Deadly Spanish Inquisition. In the second bedroom closet, my personal secret room, I will develop film and clip up future photos of my personal torture scenes so I can relive each fantasy represented as often as I desire.

ASYLUM - 2ND FLOOR LUNACY

All ten entertainment rooms, my performance rooms, on the second floor will be constructed and designed with peepholes and recording devices for my visual and audio pleasure. I'm adept with the latest, sophisticated technology and I can ask Albert if I need any additional electrical advice or more of his services. Albert will also install secret monitor cameras in each of the rooms that I will be able to peek at my guests from the front desk and my private quarters. There will be a hidden security camera at the front and back doors. The surveillance cameras will provide significant observation for visual stimulation for me to relive all the torturous deaths I'll experience in the future. This critical introduction is only a glimpse of my future here at the already, infamous Blue Pine. Soon, an on-going, dramatic, sinful and wicked theatrical production will unfold and be described in my journal before, during or after each episode. When I'm not working in my little theaters, I will thrive on reading this beloved Journal.

At 8:00 AM Tuesday morning, my extraordinary operation started on time. I closed my eyes, took a deep breath, and hoped for the best. Gerry, the plumber, Albert the electrician and Joe, the carpenter, all arrived on time. I was getting a little anxious when I took Gerry up to the 3rd floor. I went to the 1st bedroom suite in the front of the house, handed Gerry my drawing and explained I wanted him to put a modest sink, toilet and tub in that room which would be mine. I also told him I wanted an update to the full bath down the at the other end of the hall for guests. Nothing fancy, plain was enough.

I realized I was at least one carpenter short if I want to expediate this plan, so I hired another man from the Daily News who showed up Thursday. He was an Englishman named Harry, so I was able to establish a great rapport with him. That was the best news since the project commenced, because a fellow Englishman would understand I was a kinky bloke. I wanted to make sure he was open-minded to bizarre requests, so I also if he had read '120 Days of

Sodom' or 'Sodom and Gomorrah' by Marcel Proust. To my delight his answers were all a yes. His wife was an avid reader and she loved Proust, so she read to him at times while they were drinking on the porch on weekends. Maybe Harry and his wife were into Sado-masochism. I thought to myself, this has been too good to be true. I took the risk of discussing my diverse agenda with Harry. I told him I was a kinky prankster, and I was anticipating entertaining and fooling friends and guests with my weird creations. Harry didn't flinch at all; in fact, he thought it was funny and was eager to begin working.

I'm going to detail more about the preliminary construction necessary for each of the ten torture rooms. I put Joe and Albert together on a one-man elevator towards the back of the house, telling them the elevator must go from the basement to the 3rd floor. Harry started on a flight of stairs that went to a door that opened up to nothing but a brick wall. He got a big laugh out of that one and to my satisfaction had it built in three days. Harry & I were going to get along.

Harry's next project was to put up a fake, sound absorbing partition wall in all ten rooms on the 2nd floor, 3 feet out from one, inside structure. This is where I chose to model part of a torture room after Holmes' infamous Murder Castle. Each wall would be iron plate lined and have additional insulation to secure soundproofing. Soundproofing these rooms was paramount. The soundproofed walls would be built back-to-back to the room next door, and a door was to be installed at one end of each partition wall. In the 3-foot space between the structure wall and fake wall, there would be a trap door in the floor with a chute that could channel a large mass passed down through it to the basement. I convinced Harry the chutes were for garbage or trash that would empty into a huge bin at the bottom. The puzzled carpenter tilted his head, gave a smirk, and got right to work on the 4th day constructing the walls, door frames and chutes. The chutes had trap doors and mounting those doors on the floorboards took much longer than planned, but all that construction was finished within a month by Harry with Andy's help.

Meanwhile, the bathroom plumbing, and installation of the elevator was still in process. Gerry was working as hard as possible sometimes after dark. In the meantime, I gave a major project to Harry, Joe and Andy when he had time. They had to work with Albert on the elevator, which was the major, complicated and challenging job, but it had to be done. I desperately needed an elevator to operate the Blue Pine as a guest house. I had to have an elevator for other reasons, too. I counted on the four men, in spite of problems and setbacks, to figure the best way to proceed. Waiting for parts and material, the elevator task became a nightmare and wasn't completed for two months. That set the whole plan back.

After Andy finished installing insulation between the walls, I had him install the same insulation on the wood floors of the ten rooms, then raise the new floor up about 10". The same ten rooms on the 2nd floor also had to be carpeted to absorb and stifle all sounds, including human screams, banging on doors and loud equipment noises. The space beneath the raised floor was to hide bodies quickly for emergencies. All rooms, including the two guest rooms would have a small 8x10 framed, one-way mirror and peepholes strategically placed on two walls. One on the inside wall and another from the hall looking in under a framed art piece.

I gave each room on the 2nd floor, a room number with a themed name so I could remember what theme went to what room number. I may appear to be a copycat killer if some readers are familiar with H.H. Holmes hotel business. We have many differences and some similarities. I'll leave that observation up to the people who find my journal. The truth of the matter is, I do look somewhat like Holmes but I'm much more attractive and debonair. I admit, occasionally I have felt like his phantom protégé, but I take pride in my originality. I am unique. However, I do admire his work, ingenuity and tenacity.

I'm going to detail more about the preliminary construction necessary for each of the ten torture rooms. I put Joe and Albert together on a one-man elevator towards the back of the house, telling them the elevator must go from the basement to the 3rd floor. Harry started on a flight of stairs that went to a door that opened up to nothing but a brick wall. He got a big laugh out of that one and to my satisfaction had it built in three days. Harry & I were going to get along.

Meanwhile, the bathroom plumbing, and installation of the elevator was still in process. Gerry was working as hard as possible sometimes after dark. In the meantime, I gave a major project to Harry, Joe and Andy when he had time. They had to work with Albert on the elevator, which was the major, complicated and challenging job, but it had to be done. I desperately needed an elevator to operate the Blue Pine as a guest house. I had to have an elevator for other reasons, too. I counted on the four men, in spite of problems and setbacks, to figure the best way to proceed. Waiting for parts and material, the elevator task became a nightmare and wasn't completed for two months. That set the whole plan back.

SANCTUARY + 3RD FLOOR GUEST ROOMS

My private quarters, a two-room suite is located on the third floor. It's at the front of the house so I can have a clear view of the front yard and entrance to the Blue Pine during the day and night. The three, overnight Guests rooms are on the opposite end of the third floor towards the back of the house where the original stairway is located. I had the carpenters rebuild the stairs, bypassing the second floor. The new, exclusive elevator goes from my suite down to the basement. The elevator entrance on the first floor is disguised behind a sliding bookcase, so no one else knows there's an elevator in the house. For my restricted use only.

The Blue Pine has a doorbell I could hear in my suite and throughout the house. I keep an audio tape recorder and Brownie camera in my room, also a duo set behind the front desk and another pair in the basement.

I turned my closet into a dark room where I develop macabre photos. I have a double bed, a large dresser, an armoire and a padded chair. In the other closet in my suite, there are two peep holes for observation into a guest room so I can watch what's going on when I care to be amused.

My room's décor has dark green wallpaper with a beige, scallop design, old Victorian furniture, elaborate swagged beige drapes, beige woodwork with a green and cream-colored oriental carpet. Obviously, it had served as the master bedroom and it's fine for me. I keep all of my wardrobe and Victorian garb hung neatly in my alternative closet. My suite is comfortable and suitable for escaping away from the grizzly life I live. This is my sanctuary.

The official guest rooms are rather simple. The only suggestion of the Victorian era in those rooms is the molding, doors and windows. The furniture in those rooms was too old, soiled and damaged, so Andy took it all to the dump, then went to a couple of charity shops to pick up a bed, dresser, lamp and nightstand for each room. I took a trip into Bangor on a Saturday to buy towels, blankets and sheets at Sears, Roebuck for the guests and for me plus sets of traditional, simple drapes for the guest rooms. I won't encourage anyone to stay more than a few days, or a week at most. I don't want anyone to be here long enough to get wise to my covert operation.

DEVIL'S DUNGEON - BASEMENT

I call the basement, the 'Devil's Dungeon' or Zone 666, depending on my temperament at the time. I think the name is fitting because according to literature, murderers are referred to as evil and monsters, because of their heinous crimes. The worst, most sinister of my evil ventures now will take place on the 2nd floor and in the basement.

In more detail, I was pleased to find the basement was equipped with a mortuary cooler that had three spaces, a cremation chamber, 2 stainless steel embalming tables, a body lift and 2 cadaver carts. To my satisfaction, it is also supplied with a fair assortment of embalming tools including a brain knife, an eight-inch knife instead of a 1-inch scalpel blade, a bone saw and Hagedorn needle. I had brought my own bag of tools which included a hammer with a hook, pruning shears instead of surgical bone cutters, a Stryker saw and toothed forceps. I bought most of my tools at a hardware store because they are cheaper, stronger, have longer blades and I learned in the New York funeral home, they do a better job. I will be well equipped here at the Blue Pine for any gruesome act I choose. The mainstream doesn't know many medical examiners shop at restaurant supply warehouses and hardware stores to save a lot of money.

Later, when all necessary construction is completed on the three floors above, the worker I trust the most will be working on custom equipment for the basement. The mandatory, first assignment will be hiding the door that goes down to the basement from the 1st floor. I will give instructions for a covert entrance and exit for emergencies and my use only. The present door will be removed. I will have a simple, 8-foot tall, 4-foot-wide bookcase hung on a sliding track attached invisibly on the back of the top of the bookcase. It will appear to be stationary because the sliding track will be locked conveniently below, eye level on the inside and outside. I will be able to slide the bookcase to the side to enter or exit the stairway to the basement. The two windows in the basement will be filled with cement blocks and that underground floor will be soundproofed. My covert workshop will serve many purposes including an escape from reality.

Most likely, it will be Harry I allow access and to know more of my deviant secrets. He will get my sketches to convert the autopsy table to a duo functioning bondage and stretching rack. It will be as unique as I am and one-of-a-kind.

Recently, I bought two large metal water troughs from a farm supply store out in the country. One will be filled with acid for dissolving flesh, hair and organs off a cadaver and the other will be filled with quicklime if I can find any for purchase. Following my murder scenarios on the 2nd floor, most cadavers will be dumped into the room's chute and dropped down into the murky dungeon.

Other items ordered for the basement dungeon will be here in a few days and then my artistry of performing torture and murder will commence at the Blue Pine Guests Inn. It's been a few months since my last adventure, so my latest fantasies have become blurred; my souvenirs aren't powerful anymore. If I do not receive a guest to my liking, coming into the Blue Pine soon, I will be compelled to go hunting. However, since I've owned this multi-faceted, comfortable, well-equipped structure, I have preferred to take advantage of my options and privacy right here instead of taking the risks I expose myself to hunting on the outside.

CHAPTER 14

PAULINE'S DISTURBING DIARY

Flashing back, after the workmen departed on the first workday, when I was alone, I decided to search through every nook and cranny of the interior of my new dwelling. My curiosity always got the best of me. Oddly enough, when I was going through Sneed's master bedroom, I was surprised to find a small, tattered diary tucked safely and discreetly behind the massive headboard. It had been the secret property of Pauline M. Sneed. In cursive handwriting, she had kept a memoire about her marriage with Bartholomew. I took the upstairs my room and read every bit of it before going to sleep. If that diary had been found by anyone else, the confessions Pauline wrote about would have surely turned this quaint town upside down. If Mr. Sneed was still alive and this diary had been found by a cleaner or maid, he may have been facing a high-profile jury trial. I am going to copy the most disturbing contents of Pauline's diary in a word for word account. I'm completely impressed with Pauline's fascinating details about her married life with a mad mortician. I am starting to wonder if all funeral undertakers have a deplorable dark side like my father.

Pauline writes, quote:

"I don't know if anyone will ever find my diary and read it, but if someone does, I'm sure I will be dead and buried before then and that will be my saving grace. I decided to start writing about my marriage to Bartholomew, hoping writing would help me cope with my unbearable living situation"

We got hitched in Bucksport in 1921, the same year we bought this funeral parlor and changed the name from Your Friendly Funeral Parlor to the Blue Pine Funeral Home. When I dated Bart, he was such a gentleman, educated, suave and compassionate. I saw nothing that made me think he had skeletons in his closet. I married him after I graduated from college with my nursing degree. Bart was a professor at the University of Maine in Orono.

We moved to Briggstown, bought this turnkey business, moved in and a few months later is when everything changed. It was like I married Dr. Jekyll but ended up with an evil Mr. Hyde. For thirty years I kept this secret to myself, only writing about it here. Being a nurse, I should have recognized the red flags and left the marriage before a year's end, being in love with Bart sugar coated those signs until it was too late. I know I have suffered from a psychological condition from repeated on-going mental and physical traumas from my husband Bart. Someday in the future someone in the medical field may evaluate my issue as a stress or psychological disorder. I never told my conservative, religious parents, my hot-headed, biker brother or my loving best friend Rose because I didn't want any of them to think I was either hysterical, stupid or insane. For sure they would all think I was mentally ill to have stayed in this marriage for a moment once I realized who Bart really was and they would have been right. To save face and go with the traditional marriage which frowned on divorce, I chose to suffer instead for the horrible mistake I made marrying Bart. I believe I was punishing myself for being stupid. Here it is over a year into this madness and I'm still living a lie, pretending I'm someone other than Pauline.

It's August 26, 1922. Just two years ago on this day, the long, campaign fight for woman suffrage was starting to change the rights for some women. I decided to start my memoire on this special day, August 26, so that some day after I'm gone, everyone will know the truth about our marriage and maybe it will be published. If the lady or gent who finds my diary should decide to have my confessions put in print, it may save a few women; even if it saves just one woman from a life of misery that should never happen, it would be worth it.

Everything at the beginning of our marriage appeared normal until I started hearing him say things I didn't expect nor understand why. Bart started being dictatorial in a verbally abusive tone. I thought our business was getting to him, so I excused his behavior in my mind when he lashed out at me or ordered me to do something instead of asking. I blamed it on the strain and bizarre tasks that comes with preparing a corpse. Most take for granted the job of a mortician, but unless you are involved in it yourself, you can't imagine what it's really like being around dead and disfigured cadavers every day. Of course, we in the field of medicine and those in the funeral business become desensitized, but sometimes the preparations of certain bodies are nastier and more disgusting in appearance, odor and clean up. But that's not what I'm writing about. Another thing has been bothering me. Mr. S. has been going out at night, sometimes for a few hours and not telling me where he's going or where he has been. When I ask he says in a cruel tone,

"None of your business, puppy."

That first year passed so quickly, being busy, I didn't realize I was being sucked up into a sub-culture slowly but steadily by a man I didn't know anymore. Bart started calling me puppy in private instead of Pauline. He'd say,

"I want my poor little puppy to get me a cup of coffee."

If I didn't drop what I was doing and quickly get his coffee, he would grab my arm, pull me down on his lap and spank me vigorously, until I cried out and begged him to stop. Orders, criticisms and punishments escalated from mild to severe in a short length of time, due to Bart's progressively intense, cruel behavior. I learned to adjust to the hard, painful spankings and he had me believe it was necessary, but I never liked it or being called puppy. That never sat well with me, but I tolerated it for the sake of keeping peace. I have become deathly afraid of Bart.

For our first Christmas last year, in December 1921, he bought me sexy, red lingerie, a blindfold and brought home a bag of rope from the hardware store. I didn't think anything too strange about my gifts, because his pretty wrapped gift box also included an elegant Elgin watch. On Christmas morning, Bart ordered me to model the lingerie. I did without a fuss, but not quickly enough, so over his lap I went. The new year started with more demands, orders, chores and discipline. He started with a little at a time and before I understood what was happening, he had brainwashed me and manipulated me into what he wanted. When I realized Mr.

Bartholomew Sneed was a sexual sadist, a wolf in sheep's clothing and… I drew my own conclusions from having read about the French libertine and writer, the infamous Marquis de Sade and through my research on Richard von Krafft-Ebing. This year, when Bart's discipline, he called it, (I called it his violent outbursts) got more severe, I secretly went to the library on my way home from shopping to research more about it. That package wasn't the only gift I received. I don't have much time to write secretly, but I will date and document as much as possible from January 1923 on.

January 1, 1923

The holidays were very different this year. Santa's big gift for me was a casket all of my own. It was an expensive bronze casket. Bart said it was the best on the market and I should appreciate it. I was shocked and confused. I couldn't imagine what that was for. I thought he was going to kill me, and I'd be buried in it. I'm writing this morning because Bart got intoxicated last night and he's still in bed recovering from a splitting headache.

June 2, 1923

I haven't been able to write since January. Bart doesn't let me out of his sight for any significant amount of time. Business here at the Blue Pine has slowed down. Maybe there will be more weddings than funerals. It's 12:00 AM and I'm still awake and alone. My life this year has taken a 180-degree turn for the worse. Bart insists I call him 'sir', yes sir, no sir, thank you sir, and please may I sir. He makes me wear see through lingerie after we close at night. Now, when I displease his whims, I'm ordered to get into my casket. He closes the top for 30 minutes and I breathe through a plastic tube. I feel I'm being buried alive or if he is giving me a clue of my demise.

One night recently, he left me for a few hours and left the house. I tried desperately to get out until I realized he had locked it. I wore myself out and fell asleep wondering what he was doing out late at night? This year, he started demanding oral sex which I don't like. He almost chokes me every time and laughs when my eyes tear, I moan in pain and gag. This is not what I want but I have no choice. My future looks more very every day. I want to leave but I can't.

October 20, 1927.

Four years have flown by. I haven't had access to my diary for too long a time, but I think this is going to be a sign of the future. Sir keeps me in sight all day and night. At times, he ties me to a chair in the basement while he's embalming a stiff. I'm ordered not to wear underwear at home. I'm ordered to be his goffer, his cook, his sex object, and his anger relief. I have become totally dependent on Sir. I have no time for myself alone anymore because he doesn't permit it. I'm smart enough to know I've developed a psychological and emotional bond with him. I wanted to run away five years ago, but now I don't want to. I don't like what I've become, but I can't live without Sir. I've become used to the violence and humiliation. I live in fear and dependency on Bart and isolation from the rest of the world. He ostracized the only friendship I had in Briggstown. Rose.

May 7, 1940

I don't see the need to sneak around to write anymore. It's become more intense here over the last ten plus years. Sir's demands and his physical and emotional violence has gotten worse. The 1930's was a decade of horror and despair. I've been forced to do sexual things with dead people. The first time, he had me kiss the corpse, put my tongue in her cold, gross mouth. I vomited all over her hair and face and of course, I was ordered to clean it up. He threatened me that I would have to lick it up, but he laughed and didn't make me do it. His threats are as demeaning and frightful as his orders. I've been forced to watch Sir have sex with cadavers, too. Other times, he made me lay across the body of a dead female so he could penetrate both of us. This cadaver was still slightly warm when she arrived.

One pretty female he became extra fond of. He finally told me he had picked one of them up on a dark street in downtown Bangor where ladies of the night hung out. Another, at the big trucker's station further south of Bangor. He said he killed each of them and brought each home when I was locked up in my casket. Putting 2+2 together, I realized his nighttime disappearances were for finding a whore, so I asked him if that was true. To my surprise, he said, "yes". That was all, just yes. What was left of my rationality told me that now, since he had confessed his evil ways, he would never trust me or let me go. I was in captivity for the rest of my life. I was Sir's slave and property forever. He was a sexual sadist, a psychopath and most likely a vicious murderer and there was nothing I could do to stop him.

March 18, 1947

Everything is still the same except for a couple of changes. Sir went out tonight. I was put in my casket again with the tube, but when I heard the car start up this time, I figured I'd be alone for at least a couple of hours, so I used my bare feet and pushed up and hard against the inside of the top, but it didn't open all the way. I was shocked to see he had forgotten to lock it, so I plunged my feet upward with all my strength and the top opened far enough for me to squeeze out and escape. Getting out with my hands bound was tricky, but I was determined to write in my dairy. When Sir sees my footprints on the cream-colored satin lining, I assume I will be scolded beyond anything I've suffered before. I was not able to climb back in my casket, so I know things are going to be brutal when he returns. I must run up to the bedroom and write before he comes home. I thought I had a few hours if he went to Bangor, but I was wrong. He went to the Long Drink for less than an hour. I heard my car pull into the driveway. The monster is home, so I stopped writing and ran down to sit near my casket.

July 12, 1952

I was punished beyond one's imagination for days after my escape from the casket. I was forced to do despicable, unmentionable sex acts with dead bodies, so terrible I will not write about it. I was locked in my casket for 24 hours without food or water. Once, right after my escape, he pulled back the top and put a cold, stinking, dead cat in with me and closed the lid. I screamed and yelled and cried out; thought I would surely lose my mind. The last five years, I've been living in a horror movie. This poor little puppy has lost reality with life. I can't function on any normal level or do chores with efficiency. I have become a spiritless product of my abuse. I am of little use to the evil monster I married, so I believe that my days on earth are coming to an end soon. He has been threatening to kill me over the last few weeks if I didn't shape up and do a better job and I know he's serious. If I'm found dead, you should look at Mr. Bartholomew Sneed because he is the culprit who put me in an early grave. He is a murderer. He is a mentally ill, perverted and has been a prolific killer since about 1922, or maybe even before I met him. I have survived this hell, a thirty-year nightmare in total captivity. I know I am doomed to die this year, and I wonder what method he will use. This week I have felt sleepy, with dizziness, headaches and nausea to the point I've thrown up. My heart rate is irregular, and Bart's been cooking dinner lately. I wonder if he's been trying to poison me. God help me."

CHAPTER 15

ANDREW'S VIEW OF PAULINE'S DIARY

"That was the last entry of Pauline's writings in her diary before she died. Towns folk were told she died of a cardiac arrest, but after reading her diary, I am certain old man Sneed killed his wife. I know I'm also a perverted psychopath killer and necrophiliac, but I had never heard of or thought of the likes of things Bartholomew did to his wife. Sure, I like sex with corpses, but I've never forced anyone else to participate in my twisted desires. Have I missed out on something?

Pauline was clearly not in favor of the sadistic rituals Sneed forced on her. She was swept up into his web of deception and manipulation where she couldn't think for herself. His sadistic, abnormal narcissism was in a category unlike mine. It was relieving to learn I wasn't as deviant as someone else and fascinated to find out there are a sundry of necrophiliacs. Pauline's diary answered some questions plaguing me for many years. I'm thankful I was the lucky lad that found her diary first. I was ecstatic to read in Pauline's diary. I had been thinking I was the only American killer who was also a necrophiliac since Holmes. I don't feel so alone knowing there has been another monster right here from this area who was worse than me. At least in my opinion Sneed was more evil than me.

When I was snooping through the shelves in the basement, I found a container with a residue of cyanide. It had a warning label on it, and I recognized what it was, but didn't think much of it at that time. I knew it was used for killing ants, sometimes rats, so I figured Sneed had had an infestation of some kind. But with the symptoms Pauline described in her dairy, I'm sure she died of chronic cyanide poisoning. I was certain Sneed had killed before Pauline. If so, he would have possibly been a murderer of many but with the perfect cover up of a funeral home where he could have disposed of his victims in his crematorium. I surely agree with that.

I don't have the filter to feel sorry for the unhappy nurse-wife, but it's unfortunate she suffered a life of torment and torture. I've often thought of getting married, but I don't want to sacrifice my freedom to satisfy my desires for constant intimate companionship with the same woman. It's easier with part time women in my life. Sometimes I murder them, sometimes I tell them to get out. I tell all of them up front I have no intention of getting serious.

Now, more is coming back to me. The coroner told Mel, he found Pauline's cool body in a coma with blue lips and face. Sneed had called the police and told them when he came up from the embalming room, he found her lifeless body on the bathroom floor. I think after she croaked, he made one last use of her warm, unconscious body and went back down to the embalming room and didn't call the police for a couple of hours. That's what I would have done. She was pronounced dead on site and was sent to the hospital morgue for an autopsy. The next morning her corpse was sent back to her husband's funeral home per his request. Pauline's death must have triggered something even more sinister in the mortician's mind. That's when he started showing bizarre behavior in public.

I believe Pauline had survived that wrenched, brutal and tragic relationship as long as she did because of her religious beliefs and strong will. Also, she spared her family and friends the anguish and misery of knowing about her own pain. I believe she was a fine woman, one that Sneed did not deserve. God rest her soul.

CHAPTER 16

PREDISPOSED TO BE A 'SADIST'

I'd like to give you a better understanding of why I am who I am. My interest in dead bodies came from years living in a funeral home from childhood and working at a morgue, but my passion for inflicting torture may have a double-fold component with my upbringing and excessive exposure to death.

For one, I had an egotistical mother who terrified me with religion and punishments daily. Her critical, abusive treatment happened mostly when dad was at work. She was a protestant, Baptist fanatic. I didn't know as a child why religious fundamentalism was a parasitic ideology that takes control of the brain commanding individuals to think and act like they are told. My mother tried endlessly to brainwash me to destroy my capability to think independently, but I had a strong mind and will even as a child. I turned my mind off to her consistent, forced influence, despite her continued manipulation to mold me into the perfect, wholesome, religious son.

I was cute, intelligent, and smart beyond my years, and ahead of my peers in school. She wanted to show me off to other parents and relatives, but it tortured me because I was shy and wanted to be left alone. Mother kept expecting more and more from me, sometimes becoming physically violent with a paddle, yard stick or anything that was close and handy. She was authoritarian, cold and aloof to me. She often threatened me, made me feel shame or guilt and called me names if I got a B or an A- on a paper or report card. I grew up angry, keeping the dark secret to myself to spare my father the grief. His job was stressful enough. I fantasized taking the paddle from mum and turning the tables on her to give her a taste of her own medicine. Fortunately, I was able to restrain myself during childhood. However, years of restraining that desire for retaliation and revenge may have programmed me for sadistic and violent tendencies. I read in the library, my restraint from seeking revenge may not lead to sadism, but it could contribute to a child's behavioral and emotional development which could influence future behavior.

Another reason could be all the bullying and rejection I suffered from other students at school, probably out of envy of my grades, my proper English accent and maybe I looked weird to them with my white shirt and polka dot bow ties. No other kids dressed like that, but mother insisted I shouldn't look like all the other boys, because she said I was different from the rest. I didn't want to look different or stand out. It was embarrassing.

Consequently, I grew up without empathy or care about anyone's feelings. In high school, I filled out weight and stature wise, and my attitude started changing accordingly. I went from being bullied to being a bully to those who appeared weak looking and were gullible underdogs. I lied to get my way, never taking any blame for anything. After puberty I wanted nothing to do with girls. I have never been interested in any female unless she was deceased, pretty and still warm. It is rare to receive them like that.

Once, out of pure, untamed curiosity, I raped a prepubescent, nine-year-old blonde boy who had been killed by a car. I had been curious since Proust about experiencing sodomy with a boy. To me it felt similar to a young virgin female. A twelve-year-old blonde girl came into the morgue in Southern Maine after she had been in a cooler at the hospital after she was killed by a hit and run motorist. I hated the feeling of a cold vagina, but I got pleasure knowing I had raped a sweet, cute, little, twelve-year-old virgin. Dead or alive, I know that makes me a pedophile.

Not to sound narcissistic, but I am, I'm also a brilliant, goal driven, successful psychopath. I consider myself a hedonistic killer with no feelings of empathy, guilt or remorse. I learned a lot about myself in courses at college which helped me understand who and why I was me. I must have control. It's all about conquer, power and control.

CHAPTER 17

INNKEEPER'S FORMAL FASHION & ETIQUETTE

I was pondering today, speculating if the people who find my journal will try to imagine what a deranged man like me looks like and dresses like. Whether I'm short, tall, fat or sinewy. I'm going to describe myself in more detail.

I'm a refined English gentleman. I'll explain that in a moment. I am 6'2" tall and slim. I have pale skin, black, wavy hair and hazel eyes. I have always been fond of the late 19th century, English Gentleman's dapper look. With my education and upbringing, I can wear it well.

After college out on my own, I started growing facial hair. For the last several years after trial and error, I finally accomplished the look I wanted. I have a stylish 19th century, Englishmen's mustache with a thin, one-inch twist at both ends which curve slightly upwards and stand out against my short beard and adjoining sideburns. I consider my facial hair style to be classic and debonaire and it has a lot of maintenance. It must be cleaned daily and shampooed with conditioner twice a week. I make my own mustache wax using bees wax to keep its shape in order. I have received compliments from both men and women, so I'll keep it as it is.. Every morning, I have a bathroom routine, then I pick out my clothes for the day.

My British mum was unbearable with her religious views, but she taught me Victorian etiquette; polished manners and the social graces of sophistication so that I could travel in high society with the image and behavior of a gentleman. Refined taste is shown in impeccable dress and manners. I didn't like all the training, which included the art of intellectual conversation and proper speech, but my mother insisted so I had to submit to learning it as well. I also learned how to bow and tip my hat. I eventually mastered the art of being charming, respectful and poised, not knowing how much it all would come in handy someday.

Alas, I will put to good use all of my childhood training here at the Blue Pine Guest Inn. What better disguise than having an image of upper, social status and privilege when operating a Victorian mansion as a guest house. Ladies should be smitten by a handsome bloke dressed in formal Victorian fashion with impeccable speech, an authentic British accent and proper etiquette. Thank you, mum.

Predictably, my fashionable wardrobe will be as elegant as my etiquette. Since my teenage years, I had dressed like the average American man in suits and ties. Being the new owner and host of the classic, Blue Pine Guest Inn here in Briggstown, it will be my first opportunity to dress in the fashions I like the most. I will wear my tailored three-piece suits and ties on casual certain occasions, but greeting guests at the door of this stately, Victorian mansion, I will wear a vintage tailcoat with a high-collared shirt and waistcoat with a cravat and pocket watch. My shirt has layers of ruffles from the collar down my chest and on the edge of the cuffs. I will wear a top hat that I will tip to a lady who comes to my door and white gloves on formal occasions. I have been picking up pieces of clothing and accessories throughout my adult years and saved them for when the time would come, I could proudly wear them. I will continue to look for more vintage Victorian clothing, yet it is rare to find them in good shape these days. I may have to resort to a custom tailor however, what I have will be fine for now.

I chose heughs of maroon paint and cream color shades for my color scheme in the reception area and tearoom to compliment the best tailcoat and shirt I have. Everything must look proper and with a theme. This is how Mr. Andrew Webb will be dressed when I meet and greet guests who come into the Blue Pine. Like I've said before, I don't look nor act like my boring peers, nor do I care to do so.

CHAPTER 18

ANDREW'S FATEFUL FLASHBACK

All necessary construction, plumbing and electrical were finalized in 90 days. For me, patience became a virtue, because I had to stay here most of the time to keep an eye on my workers and give instruction as the projects went along. I was frustrated and getting too anxious to be tied up in this mansion with no privacy or access to do my sexual desires.

Around the sixty-day mark, one Saturday night, I went to the Long Drink and met a woman who was painted up, had a big, black, bouffant hairdo, a tight, short skirt and tall skinny heels. I knew she was a lady of the night when the bartender Mel introduced us. Before I sat down, I detected Sheila took an immediate liking to me, flirted and rubbed her pointed, high heel against my thigh. I could have easily reciprocated an interest, but she was well known by too many locals, so I had to ignore her advances. Had I weakened and taken her out of there, I might have sealed my fate and never had the experience of operating my new business. I didn't trust myself to not get into trouble.

I did speak with her, but after one quick brew, I had to make an excuse and get the hell out of the bar before my depraved desires took control of my common sense. I ran to my car shaking and when I got in the car I couldn't drive before I masturbated through my slacks to get some relief from my disappointment. That was a close call. I couldn't afford to make any stupid mistakes. I had come this far with my new life's future, and I didn't dare ruin that. My days at the Blue Pine may eventually be numbered, but I hoped this new venture would last at least another ten years and I don't want to finish my journal behind bars.

CHAPTER 19

WELCOME-BLUE PINE GUEST INN

A year has passed since the mansion's construction projects were completed and became usable, but I kept detailed reports of my deadly adventures in my journal. I finally opened the business in July 1953. I had a significant sign planted near the end of the driveway. It said, 'Welcome, Blue Pine Guest Inn, $15 per night, Vacancy; Register 4:00 PM – 9:00 PM. I had several guests for one or two nights during the first few weeks, but I had to wait until I was convinced by a tourist's story or a server seeking a pit stop, that he or she wouldn't be risky and not missed. I had to be picky and interview each guest.

I dressed in my dapper, Victorian tailcoat outfit and greeted everyone in the parlor or at the front desk. I asked a few preliminary questions before I decided to take a guest into the tearoom where I continued an informative conversation and offered a glass or two of wine. If someone refused my tearoom invitation, I promptly said we had just received a call prior to their arrival, so I had no vacancy this week.

My interview included these basic questions. Where are you from? Are you sightseeing or visiting family and friends? Married? May I have a contact number for emergencies? How long are you planning to vacation (or work) in this area?

Rarely, I disqualified a potential guest from a gut feeling; occasionally, I welcomed a guest who didn't pass the interview, strictly for boarding. My select guests, after a five to ten-minute visit in the tearoom, I knew who I would allow to rent a room for the night on the third floor, or who I fancied for fun on the 2nd floor. I relied on my good judgement. It usually proved successful.

At last, I chose a transient fellow, a young man barely twenty-one, who came up to these parts looking for seasonal work. His family lived in Pennsylvania, but they weren't close; he hadn't talked to them in months and had no girlfriend. Nobody knew where he was, not even a friend. It was about 5:00 PM. I gave Robert three glasses of red wine and showed him to his fate, his room on the 2nd floor.

My first scene of thrills in the Blue Pine was on the menu that night and I was salivating with delight and anticipation. Before I go into detail about the scenes that have already transpired in my murder mansion, I must confess this once more. I achieve my supreme source of joy and sexual pleasure watching and listening to my victims' suffering in pain and anguish.

You have noticed I have an admiration for H.H. Holmes and respect for his work, but my torture rooms, my presentation, my character and my modus operandi are quite different than what went on in his murder castle in the early 1890's. Authorities may label me a 'copycat' murderer if I'm apprehended, but I'm not. If I was, I would have bought or built a big hotel, made my torture rooms like all of his and adopted his hotel operation. I did not. I have my own individual requirements and novel torture equipment. We are different.

It's time to describe some of my monstrous pleasures that took place on the 2nd floor of the Blue Pine over the first year I was in operation. You will see what I'm talking about when you read how I precisely performed. The only room where I intentionally copied a concept from H.H. Holmes was in Room 201. I dedicated 201 to Holmes because of his infamous status for being America's first infamous killer. I have always wondered if I will go down in history someday as one of America's most notorious killers. I would be honored for that recognition and reputation.

CHAPTER 20

AGONY & ECSTACY HOMICIDES 2ND FLOOR

Room 201 - H.H. Holmes' Gas Chamber

One of my personal favorites is the H.H. Holmes Chamber, because it's the only room in the Blue Pine on the 2nd floor that closely resembles America's first and foremost, H.H. Holmes. It's a 'Gas Chamber-Asphyxiation Room.' Albert had installed four extremely dangerous, leaking, Victorian gas lamps on the walls of that peculiar, small room which turned it into the perfect asphyxiation chamber. This may be my favorite torture room.

I turned the evil gas fixtures on from a switch in the next room. I unlocked the door, stepped back and said my guest, "After you, sir." Robert briskly walked through the door and over the threshold with a big smile on his face until he saw no bed or furniture. I quickly shut the door behind him and locked him in. That was easy but he turned around immediately, pushed me aside and started banging on the door to let him out, but of course I ignored his cries of fright and pleas to be released. I was forced to give him a quick chop to his neck to stun him so I could slip out of the room and lock the door. I took the notepad and pen out of my secret, inside pocket to take notes of Robert's misery and pain. Death by gas is extreme torture and delightful to watch through the 2-way mirror because it can take several minutes. Robert was conscious enough to continue to bang and kick on the heavily sealed door of Room 201. I watched him gasp and struggle to breath for about three minutes while he was trying to escape out of a locked window until the deadly fumes overpowered his actions. He started to gag and choke, going limp and falling to the floor. Robert groaned and moaned, gulped and wheezed, no words were being screamed now. He thrashed and flailed on the floor, beating his head against the wall so hard he started to foam at the mouth then throw up. The wine he drank came out in spews of red foam among the last chunks of food he had ingested in the tearoom. He suffered for another four minutes, until he suffocated to death in a large pool of his own slime and vomit.

I'm lucky I don't get ill from such a nauseating sight, and the repulsive smell of emitted gas would soon be added to feces and urine by the time I decided to clean up the mess. I turned off the horrible gas lamps, held my breath, turned on the overhead fan and opened the only locked window in 201 which faced the back of the house. I had to clear out the nasty smells and gaseous odor, so I could return later before rigor mortis set in. In the meantime, I got some food from the kitchen and sat down in the parlor to relax and revel in that new experience while I ate some New England baked beans, salt pork, a piece of ham and a buttered biscuit. In that short time, I had worked up an appetite because of my prolonged anticipation and thrilling adrenaline rush. Everything went well and to my expectations. Room 201 was used before any of the other rooms. It was an initiation to commence the next adventures at the Blue Pine.

After dinner and a brief nap, I went to my suite to change clothes. I removed my special Victorian outfit and hung it neatly in the closet. I went back to the scene of the crime in nothing but shorts that night to get rid of the vile corpse with Vicks Vapor Rub smeared under my nostrils and a small bag of coffee beans in my pocket. I wrapped Robert's lifeless body in a large piece of plastic and dragged the bundle behind the partition wall and over to the chute, where I pushed him down into the dark tunnel. When I heard the corpse plunge into the metal bin at the bottom of the chute in the basement, I proceeded to clean up the putrid mess Robert had left. After all was done, I cleaned myself up, put on a robe, and relaxed in the parlor once again with a glass of Burgandy and a good cigar, listening to my dark, classical music by Grieg.

Before retiring to bed, I had to listen to one of my favorite classical pieces, 'The Isle of the Dead' Op.29 by Sergei Rachmaninoff. I also became intrigued with the story that went with this composition. As I remember, Sergei was deeply affected by a black and white reproduction of Arnold Bocklin's painting in Paris in 1907. The painting portrays a boat carrying a coffin to a uninhabited island, evoking themes of death and the afterlife. Rachmaninoff composed his musical interpretation of that painting. Every time I listen to this significant piece of music, this powerful, emotional symphony evokes my darkest emotions and fantasies.

Room 203 - Electric Lounge

This room hosts my creation of the Electric Chair. No hood to cover my guest's head is needed for this imposing, exclusive chair. I want to see it all, right down to the excruciating facial expressions, bubbling at the mouth and eyes bulging out with blood dripping down someone's distorted face.

A horrific scene took place in Room 203 that was another brutal homicide. It had to deal with an unexpected outcome of what happened in room 203, what I call the Electric Lounge. Jerry, who I called Jerry Boy, was the first man I experimented with in the electric chair, my old sparky.

For this unique scene, I chose a tough looking, muscular man, thirty-six, who was in Maine from West Virginia waiting for his promised, seasonal job to open in Southwest Harbor. During my second month of operation, I believed I had found the perfect male victim for the Electric Lounge. I chose distinctively because I wanted to watch this brown-haired jock cry like a baby. He acted so confident and cocky at his interview that made me eager to knock him down and make a little girl out of him. His name was Jerry Boy, but I thought of him as a little girl. It took longer to convince cocky Jerry Boy to have a stiff drink and talk him into renting a room for the night. No one from West Virginia would be impressed by my elegant décor and classical music. He was a country boy, former farm hand who didn't know about culture, much less appreciate it. He had the audacity to ask me why I was dressed up in feminine clothing. That aggravated me to anger which I had to suppress.

I put two sleep aids into his double Manhattan, with whiskey, sweet vermouth and bitters. I wanted Jerry Boy to stay here and stay awake, just get weak enough so I'd have to help him up to the 2nd floor. Within twenty minutes after drinking my deadly cocktail, he was squiffy enough and staggering a little, but I was able to get him into Room 203 without a problem. Before Jerry Boy realized he wasn't in a guest room, I had him sitting in the hard wooden chair and partially strapped in. He asked with a slur.

"What is this game we're playing, Andrew?"

I didn't answer, I continued to finish tightening the belts and straps around his torso, arms, legs and head. Finally, it hit him, this wasn't going to be a fun game. He slurred his speech again.

"Hey, wait a minute, what's going on here? This isn't funny, this isn't a joke, get me out of here! Let me out right now, you son of a bitch! Let me go!"

I remember every word that came out of Jerry Boy's angry mouth. He sobered up some but was slowly getting drowsy. I took my straight razor and shaved all the hair off his head while he thrashed and screamed bloody murder. He shook his head so much that I cut his scalp several times and blood was running down his face, cheeks and neck. I told him to shut up, relax and enjoy it, but he didn't like my humor and shouted gross obscenities at me. I didn't mind that because it increased my adrenaline and anticipation tenfold and got me going straight in the direction I sought. My grande performance began.

Poor Jerry Boy seriously freaked out watching clumps of his long locks hitting the floor in an abstract array. Soon, his shouting turned to whimpering and crying like a baby, begging me to let him go but that wasn't my ultimate plan. I was having too much fun with this bloke to consider letting up. First, I poured alcohol into the open wounds on his head, neck and face. Then I threw verbal humiliation into my act.

How's little Jerry Boy doing? You cry like a little girl, are you a little girl or a nasty bitch? Which is it? Little girl or a bitch? Talk to me sissy girl, are you in pain? Does that hurt? I'm going to rename you sissy girl. Do you like being called a sissy girl? Before he could respond, I shoved a plastic ball in his mouth. My victim was literally having a fit of rage, but I didn't hesitate for a second. I put the skull cap on Jerry Boy's bald, bloody head and attached it to the battery works. I flipped the 'on' switch, on and off a couple times at first, to give my big guest a taste of things to come. With every jolt, my prisoner, little sissy girl, screamed out in excruciating agony, crying out for help and mercy between his muffled screams. I understood every attempt he made to beg me to stop.

In a few minutes, I started leaving the electric current on for longer jolts. I didn't have a blindfold on him, so I could see when his eyeballs popped out onto his bloody face. It didn't take too long before his burning flesh started to stink. I didn't like that, but it went with the scene. Jerry Boy peed through his pants, and the smell of his pungent-smelling sweat became overpowering. I grabbed my nose plugs out of my pants pocket and shoved them into my nostrils. He started drooling, and his dribble turned to bloody slobber like a red streaming vomitus. Eventually his skin swelled and turned so red and hot that his tanned skin started weeping with oozing blisters and smelling like rotten meat frying. His mouth fell wide open when I removed the gag. I'll never forget the vision of his grizzly expression. When smoke started seeping out of the helmet, I knew Jerry's head was smoking and could possibly explode. I wasn't in favor of cleaning up brains, so I switched off the electrical current and took his pulse. He was dead. He was a sight only good for a haunted house. I was so excited I could hardly contain myself. I figured he'd croak before he became cooked to death, but I think it happened simultaneously. I took a few photos throughout the process and wrote this account in my journal. After seeing the grotesque process of the monster electric chair, I decided to use this torture for men only. For some strange reason it wouldn't excite me to see a woman fry to death. I have some scruples. I have ulterior motives for the feminine persuasions.

I was under the impression my old sparky worked well because I had more control of the apparatus. It gave me time to relish every second of the fifteen-minute scene, plus take a series of photos. I considered my evening in Room 203 a brilliant success, thanks to the workers whose joint effort made the deadly chair possible.

I had a considerable amount of pleasure and visual enjoyment watching Jerry Boy slowly cook in extreme pain. My Electric Lounge was far more entertaining and dramatic than 201's gas chamber. Cleaning up wasn't as difficult as I had expected. I released all the straps; put a large plastic bag over Jerry's head and torso and pulled him down onto the floor so I could drag him over to the chute and shove his worthless corpse down to the basement.

Later that night I inhaled a large bowl of pasta al dente, two large meatballs with buttered rolls, and washed it down with half a bottle of the 'Lady's Vintage' port wine. I needed the extra robust taste on that particular eve. After I had satiated my hunger, I lit up my pipe, took a long drag and headed for the elevator. After pasta with gravy, and a full stomach, I chose to avoid cleaning up 203 until the next morning, I just wanted to go to the basement, dispose of Jerry's body, turn off all the lights and lock it down.

I was extra logy after eating the huge Italian meal, so I took my private elevator down to the weary, cool basement. I started to drag the heavy cumbersome bag over to the refrigerator to store the corpse temporarily. I didn't feel like doing anything that night except smoke my pipe, drink the rest of the bottle of wine, read the newspaper and relax in my parlor before retiring to my quarters.

But that wasn't going to transpire so quickly. I was in for a shocker I hadn't expected. Jerry started moving in the bag and muttering which made me drop the bag and jump back! Jerry wasn't dead! He had lived through the electric volts, so I hadn't given him a strong enough jolt. Jeez! Too late for that now. Plan B had to go into motion. I distinguished my pipe. I opened the bag and Jerry deliberately and laboriously slithered out on his stomach, grumbling in pain, dripping saliva foam, blood, sweat and tear tracks as he moved out of the plastic bag like a maimed snake. I was more disappointed in myself than in Jerry's appearance. I learned later that a lot more electrical volts were needed to do the job correctly.

Out of sheer frustration and failure in 203, I had lost control. I took Jerry's feet and dragged him over to the body lift and put him in it to lift him up to the embalming table where I secured his wrists and ankles with the cuffs I had installed. But then what? I was seeing red. Something sinister, and evil took control of me. I shouldn't want anyone to read this diary after all. It shows what kind of a crazy monster I am.

Jerry was in a helpless, total daze and completely disoriented, with not enough strength to try to get away. He just looked at me with dilated pupils that stared through me like two sharp daggers. He stopped mumbling and didn't pull on his restraints. He knew he was going to die but couldn't imagine how. I said nothing to him, just stared back contemplating how to end his life permanently. Then it hit me. Ugh. Here I go again, I said out loud to myself.

I went for my autopsy tools which included my postmortem instrument set, an oscillating autopsy saw, a new 8-inch blade knife, the bread knife, rib shears and forceps. I placed them on the stainless table behind me. Jerry turned as white as a ghost when I picked up the scalpel and walked over to him. I pressed my torso against the table near his head. More beads of perspiration popped out all over his hot, red face, his whole body started shaking violently, he closed his eyes and took a deep breath. He knew I was going to make his death excruciatingly painful, but he didn't know I was going to do a brief autopsy on him while he was alive and with no anaesthesia. (British spelling). After all, I must stay in practice in case I ever work at a morgue in the future. No exam for preliminary details and health issues was necessary for Jerry.

I made a large, long Y shaped incision. When Jerry screamed out in agony, I laughed. I'm sure it sounded like the hideous laugh of a lunatic and rightfully so. Next, I used my rib shears to split his ribcage open. Now I could see his heart still beating ferociously at first, but slowing down in front of me, so I reached in and clasped my hand around his heart to feel it beat for the last time. Jerry's heart would be preserved for a memory, for a keepsake. I folded the skin back in place, not stitching it up. After putting Jerry's heart in a glass jar, I cut his scalp and pulled his scalp forward exposing the skull. Next, I used the vibrating saw to remove the top of his skull. Here, I put my bare hand into his cranium and extremely gently fondled his mushy brain. I would have kept his brain instead of his heart had Jerry been an Einstein of sorts. Then his brain would have been more appealing and valuable. I held his brain in my hand for about a minute, lightly squeezing it and for the first time I became more probing, so I carefully removed it to take a closer look. I put Jerry's grey matter into a large stainless-steel pan and delicately sliced it like a tender, juicy, rare piece of filet mignon. Carefully, slowly, almost wanting to taste it, but I threw it away. I wasn't finished with dear Jerry.

I didn't have the need or want to remove other organs. I wanted to practice flaying Jerry's corpse because the next time I get the urge for removing a person's skin as my method of torture and execution, he or she will be alive. Just so you know, flaying, being skinned alive was first documented circa 800 BC and has been a form of torture ever since in many countries however it's not popular anymore. I'm not an average person. I'm an educated and self-taught man who enjoys learning about the history of what I'm involved in. I'm about to describe the flaying of Jerry.

I'm not going to boil my captive because he's already dead so it would take all the pleasure out of seeing him suffer in the bin. I couldn't stick his corpse out in the sun, so I put two heat lamps over his body for several hours to make his skin warm and loose, so it was easier to flay, and peel it off. I started with Jerry's face like historical tradition, then his torso. I made long cuts to remove large pieces of skin by ripping it off, tearing out the nerves. The nerves hanging from the skin is a grizzly sight. If he had been alive, that would have been the level of terror and pain to inducing shock until his body went numb and he lost consciousness. I'll save the best experience for next time.

When I had enough fun with Jerry's corpse, I put on a longer plastic apron and clear goggles and cut off his limbs and head and removed his hands and feet with my bone saw to bag his remains for the dump. I never put bloody pieces in my cremation oven. Unfortunately, the oven here at the Blue Pine reminds me of those ovens at the Auschwitz-Birkenau Concentration and Death Camps I read about. I only use my oven occasionally for that reason.

Room 205 – Medieval Fair

The Medieval Fair takes me back to my history books. It's most terrifying features are a Stretching Rack & Guillotine with other crude stations around the room. I was always intrigued with the Medieval era and their methods of torture ever since high school.

I studied drawings of the Torture Rack in the library and drew a version of it for Joe to use as a blueprint. My rack had two rollers, one on each end of the six-foot bed frame and was built to be three feet off the floor. I made a pair of rope restraints for wrists and a pair for ankles, all four attached to heavy chains which were securely attached onto a wheel. One of the benefits for with use of the rack is its capacity for prolonged stretching of all four limbs of a person, slowly, a little at a time. I'm able to keep putting increased pressure on all the joints of a body until I wanted to cause all limbs to be entirely torn away from their sockets.

It was an original adventure being the executioner, turning the wheel that kept moving the rollers inch by inch tightening the ropes. I became thoroughly enchanted to witness this sort of torture of piercing and unbearable pain. When I finished tormenting my victim, I completed the dislocation of all four limbs. I took my time with this clever procedure, sometimes I kept my prisoner bound on the rack for several hours before starting the stretching process. If my victim shouted obscenities at me instead of begging to be released, I took my time pulling out their fingernails. One nail for each nasty complaint or vicious insult. Some individuals never know it's to their best interest to keep their mouth shut. During the first year, I bestowed the privilege of suffering in the Medieval Fair to two men and one woman that was wicked. I found her repulsive. Both men were missing fingernails, and one was missing something else.

A bloke named Steve came to the Blue Pine a few months after I started the business, when I was in rare form with enthusiasm and expectation. He was an impolite jerk from the beginning; he never thanked me for his overindulgence of my wine or hospitality. I don't take bad manners lightly. After he was intoxicated, I showed him up to the second floor and right into Room 205. As he stood inside the door staring at the rack with a jaw dropping face, I struck him on the back of his head with a baseball bat enough to stun him and knock him down. I helped him up to the rack, pushed him down on it with a forceful punch in the jaw and quickly tied up his wrists first. That brought him to full consciousness, so he started kicking his legs, swearing and trying to pull out of the rope cuffs. I took the hammer out from under the rack and struck his kneecaps with enough force to send him into a screaming frenzy. At last, I was able to get his ankles tied up. Steve increased his foul mouth with threats of killing me or turning me in to the police. I don't take hostile threats well, so to shut him up, I forced his mouth open with a metal, surgical mouth gag and left him there to wallow in his self-pity and bearable pain for an hour. I needed a break before the real fun began.

I went downstairs to the parlor to pick up a pair of metal tongs which I held in the fireplace until they glowed like a hot orange ember. I went back to 205, put those scorching hot pinchers into the jerk's mouth and tore out his ugly, rude tongue. Blood flew everywhere and that made me angrier with Steve, so I took my frustration out on his toenails. The excruciating pain he endured from all the tortures I gave him, caused him to have a heart attack, pass out and die. Yes, Steve died of fright, torture and unbearable pain. Dead. I put his tongue in a glass jar of formaldehyde.

Before the unpleasant cleanup, I went downstairs to the parlor to take advantage of that wine everyone else had been drinking that week and polished off the rest of a bottle sitting in front of the fireplace smoking my pipe, listening to Chopin's Funeral March and then Beethoven's Funeral March until I calmed down. I admit, I was in a dark place, a dark mood, not in a bad head, but felt something foreign. I had never performed that kind of torture on anyone before Steve, including removing a tongue. Not that it upset me or made me feel sorry for the poor jerk, but that whole scene was so severe and overwhelming that my adrenaline went on overdrive to a level I may never have experienced before that night. My head was spinning, my hands were shaking, and my lips were quivering. I didn't use Room 205 for several months after Steve.

Room 207 – Dark Carnival

I call 207 the Dark Carnival. It is the largest room, twice the size of the other rooms. I had Joe and Harry tear out one wall and make one bigger room out of two. It is made up of a crazy maze of partition walls, a long, dark crooked tunnel, mirrors at every turn, 4 doors and two short staircases that lead to nowhere. I had a good time drawing out the plans for this extreme, mysterious and bizarre creation. The purpose for this design was to observe and study humans going insane and one woman did. Since women are typically hysterical creatures, I favored this room for my chosen ladies. My favorite was Agatha.

I liked Agatha when she told me her name because it reminded me of one of my favorite English authors, Agatha Christie who was famous for her fictional, detective novels. I read 'Murder on the Orient Express' in College. This Agatha was born in England like Mr. Christie, so we had a lovely conversation in the tearoom parlor for a couple of hours. I was delighted with our conversation, so I extended her visit with me. Agatha told me she had wanted to see 'The Mousetrap' a play by Agatha Christie (1952) but probably wouldn't be that lucky. After my mind was thoroughly satisfied by our talk, and after two shots of whiskey, I became eager to proceed with my evening agenda.

I told Agatha I would show her to her room, but I took Agatha to Room 207. I was anxious to see her reaction when she was completely absorbed by my psychological mind trap. We had developed a comfortable camaraderie so there was no issue getting Agatha into 207. I told her I had built a psychological puzzle for unique entertainment for my closest friends. She believed me and went into the room with enthusiasm to play a game and have fun before retiring. I stayed in this room and locked the door behind me, though I didn't think it would be necessary. I lead my unsuspecting new acquaintance to the entrance of the maze-like puzzle and told her to start there. Willingly, she started navigating around the partition walls which were made with a myriad of six-foot tall, three-foot wide, framed mirrors and glass panes, a labyrinth leading nowhere. Some of the mirrors were made with a distortion of concave or convex to cause more confusion and instability. I took some ideas for 207 from a carnival in New York I had been to as a child. That side show, I recall was called 'The House of Mirrors.' I also remembered reading about the original hall of mirrors in the Palace of Versailles, outside of Paris, but I never got to see it. I added my own special effects to 'The Dark Carnival.' I would have called 207 'House of Mirrors', but there was much more going on in there, not just mirrors.

In the beginning, Agatha chuckled and giggled, which echoed throughout the room. She was amused at trying to figure out where to go, but the more she moved around there, I heard her laughter turn to gasps. She had two directions to choose from, but because the mirrors were all obstacles themselves, she chose the wrong path, got frightened, puzzled and lost. Agatha started to panic and cry out to me to show her the way out. Her heavy breathing and cries for help became louder and louder. It was time to turn on the blue and red spotlights and sound machine that played disturbing noises like dripping water. I sat down with my journal and started to write because the atmosphere in 207 was about to get crazy.

In a short time, Agatha started screaming out my name.

"Andrew! Andrew, help me! I can't find my way out of here! I need your help, stop this game, it's not funny anymore. I trusted you! Help me!"

At this point, Agatha was completely terrorized. I admit trapping someone in a maze of this construct is purely sadistic, psychological cruelty. I smiled from ear to ear and took a deep breath of satisfaction. I lit up one of my cigars and listened to Agatha's screams and threats turn into hysterical, horrified crying. In a few more minutes, my prisoner was huffing and choking and so full of terror it sounded like she was having a serious anxiety attack. The more she screamed, cried out and choked, the more thrilling it was for me. I was the only one who achieved an immediate feeling of enjoyment and sexual pleasure.

It became clear to me at the Blue Pine, I was a prolific, sexual sadist because I achieved extreme sexual satisfaction from inflicting torture and pain on my victims. Some day if this journal is discovered, like I wrote before, I may be noted way up there with my name beside the late and great, infamous H.H. Holmes. I have a similar depraved and sadistic character. There I go mentioning Holmes again.

I documented all of my prisoner's screams, cries and frustration, until I had heard enough. Then, I went down to the kitchen to make a ham and cheese on rye with potato chips, a pickle and a cold brew. I took my snack back up to 207 and sat down to deliberate on how I wanted to murder Agatha after she went mad. I'm not concerned about my grotesque, heinous crimes, nor am I the one and only who enjoys such antics. I cannot take Ms. Agatha to the Bellevue Psychiatric Hospital in New York City and admit her there even though it's far away from where I live because they would ask too many questions. Ha, I wouldn't anyway. All joking aside, I look forward to killing my prey after torture. Thinking what should I do to this sweet, intelligent girl after I finish lunch? Would you have any suggestions?

Time passed quickly and I may have drifted out of consciousness off and on listening to Agatha, her pleasing music to my ears. I'm awake now and ready to indulge in more horrific play. Agatha's screams had lightened up mixed with a mantra of irrational babbling and some of the strangest, deranged, bizarre things I've ever heard. I knew she had gone insane and that was my goal. I knew it wouldn't take long because she had told me she suffers from severe anxiety issues and had a nervous breakdown a few years ago. I turned off the sound machine and spotlights. It was time to find dear Agatha and put her out of misery. Her misery, my pleasure.

I had the ceiling mirrored over the maze for two reasons. One, if anyone looks up, that will make them more loco; two, I can locate where they ended up and get to them more easily with the aid of the ceiling mirrors. I was quite amused to find Agatha on the floor towards the last partition; however, she would not have been able to exit at the end. I am the only one who can make access into the maze via removing a partition from the outside. I did and what a pitiful, pathetic human I found rocking back and forth, rolling side to side, murmuring incoherently and rolling her eyes back in her head with salivate running down her pale face. This was a perfect scene for a horror movie, but it was my live, private, delicious horror show that had the expected ending. It was not an presumed ending for dear Agatha, but I couldn't have been more pleased that this complex creation delivered the goal I was looking for. A pause in my journal now, because nature is calling. I will return to indulge in Act II of this exciting movie-like scene.

An hour has passed. I had sat in the parlor to reflect on my past activities. For decades my style was first to verbally seduce my victims, strangling them with a tie and sometimes slitting their throat if they still showed signs of life. I was on a continuous murder spree for the anticipation of the hunt and gratification of the kill. I always took a keepsake of lingerie, a nylon or a piece of jewelry.

Tonight, I may decide to change my style out of repetitious boredom. This is will trip up law enforcement and forensic pros because most murderers don't change their MO. I do not want to be found. I consider myself forensically savvy as well as skilled and charismatic.

But for now, I'm going to send Agatha's stiff down the chute to the basement, my most depraved playroom and workshop. I had taped her incoherent mumbling and hissing in 207 so I could get satisfaction from hearing it again in the future. This is what it sounded like.

"Mumma, help me from your grave. Please get out of your tomb and come get me, mumma. Jesus is always busy, and I don't have time… time to wait until this world comes to an end, or maybe it has already. I don't feel well, I'm dizzy, and I want to throw up. Dammit, mumma, forgive me for disturbing you. I don't know where I am or how I got here, but I want to come home, mumma! I don't know where I am but I'm in a lot of pain. Mental pain and I cut my hands trying to escape from this nightmare! I think I'm on the brink of another nervous breakdown, so please come get me mumma!"

Then she belted out weird, deafening and pitiful screams, all on tape. When I got back into 207, I located Agatha by removing a wall, put a gag in her incoherent mouth and dragged her by her ankles over to the chute, opened the hatch and shoved her breathing, limp body through the trap door and down the chute. A couple seconds later, I heard Agatha's formidable body hit the tin tub on the basement floor with a thud and a scream. I leisurely sauntered downstairs to the parlor for a Jack Daniels, one of my good stogies, and turned on classical music for a few minutes. When I heard Agatha stumbling up the stairs from Zone 666, my break ended, and Showtime was about to begin. I met her on the stairs, halfway up and knocked her with one heavy back hand over the side and she landed halfway hanging off one of the mortuary tables on the basement's floor. I flung the rest of her plump, repellant body onto the cold, stainless steel table and strapped her down with wrist and ankle sets of leather, medical, psychiatric restraints, the best in the business. I locked all four cuffs securely and pulled a chair near to the table. I released the gag from her purplish lips that were dripping saliva. I sat down with pen in hand to listen and observe more of Agatha's bizarre but imaginative insanity. I was counting on this to spice up my journal. The moment I extracted the crude, wet and bloody mouthpiece, my injured patient began to recite her pleas for help with the small amount of strength she had left. Her eyes were so teared, lighting was dim but I knew she saw me in a blur.

"Andrew, is that you? You betrayed me you bastard! You son of a bitch, I'll kill you, I swear, I'll kill you! Let me out of here, I need a doctor, I want my mother, get my mum, and bring her here to me. She'll get even with you. She'll burst out of her tomb and find you! I'm hurt, Andrew and the devil is talking to me… he said he's going to get you because Jesus isn't ever available to help me, but I know he's on his way and he will fight with you and the devil and he will win. I know he will kill you both and take me to see mumma. Jesus just said I will be dancing with the angels soon and I'll be with my mumma, and we'll all be together in paradise, but the devil said that's not true that you and the Lord will burn in hell and I will be his sexual slave and bride for all eternity!"

I must say it was beneficial that I took some shorthand in high school because I did not want to miss any of miss Agatha's tongue. I could become fond of this sort of psychological, sadistic terror. It's an alternative form of theatre and intellectual amusement for me. But I've heard enough from this hysterical bitch, so I will put her out of her miserable misery soon, after I slowly finish my drink and smoke. Let's see. Do I want to shag her now or later? Or at all? I surely don't want to mess up those expensive restraints, so I will stuff a towel in her mouth, put a towel over her face and slit her throat. Yes, I'll take my largest, razor sharp, meat cleaver and slice her delicate little throat from one side to the other. Ah, no, that's not enough. I want to decapitate this one and put her head in my cadaver refrigerator. First time, I wanted to keep someone's head for a souvenir. Why was I getting such atrocious ideas? Oh, God, help me.

Back to my journal. I did it. About half an hour ago, I distinguished my stogie, jumped up on the shiny table, got up between Agatha's trembling legs, lifted the towel up from her face just long enough to see her frozen, panic-stricken expression, covered her face again and slammed that heavy, deadly meat cleaver down on Agatha's neck with one, precise, deliberate blow. I used such force that her head split from her torso with one chop and blood spatter flew onto the stairs, the closest door, the walls and the ceiling above and all over me. What an appealing, red fan pattern it made like an abstract art, like sinister wall art. I'm thinking, I might keep that, not clean it up tonight, maybe never and take photos of it. Since nobody else will ever be allowed in the Devil's Dungeon, the decorative blood art would be for my eyes only.

I cleaned Agatha's face carefully and thoroughly before I put her head in a plastic bag and into the cooler. I hadn't been interested in collecting heads before this, so she may be the only one.

An hour had passed since her head hit the cooler. I felt Agatha's body, and it was still warm, so I removed both sets of cuffs, placed them in the cabinet where they belong and jumped back up on the table, just like the old days, back in the funeral home in New York. I wondered how I would deal with this when the time came, because I couldn't easily get up and down off a table like this anymore.

It didn't take any time at all to get an erection even though I had never penetrated a headless corpse. Maybe the novelty of it stimulated me. I've done and seen so much that it takes a lot to entertain me these days. It's got to be the forbidden elements that also inspire me and drive me to do such horrific, atrocious murders. I went into Agatha with all the gusto and enthusiasm of a teenage boy, but even for me it was a tad repulsive without her head. I probably shouldn't put the following in print, but I will. To try something new, I got off the table before I lost my load, went to the end of the table, pulled off all my clothes and discarded them on the chair. I took the headless corpse by her arms and pulled her open, hot, blood-filled neck towards my body and rammed my big jozzer straight into her warm, bloody neck to see how that would feel. Three thrusts is all it took before I unloaded a ton of cum into

Agatha's slimy neck. I know those who will eventually read this journal are going to puke and think I'm one sick bloke but just think of it as an experiment in the name of science and sex. My opinion of that experience is… it was so freaky, so wrong, it was good, but very messy. My torso, genitals and upper legs were drenched in blood.

I took a long, hot shower directly after shagging the gory, headless cadaver. I stayed in the shower longer than usual with the water blasting against my face playing over and over what I had done, how it all felt to me now and how it would feel to me later. I wasn't convinced if I wanted the decapitation session to stay foremost on my mind as the most dominant, reminiscent fantasy. If I became extremely absorbed in my performance of Agatha's horrific demise, I'd be certain I had fallen into a much darker place than before, the darkest place a psyche could dwell. If that transpired, then for what or where would my fantasy mind be able to go to surpass shagging a bloody, decapitated corpse? I have executed my victims in many sadistic ways, but this last session opened up another Pandora's Box.

I clenched my fist tightly and pounded the tile wall, one, two, three and four so hard, I grunted with pain in my hand. Whew. I knew the answer and I wasn't going to fool myself. Once a person experiences dark, darker, or darkest and achieves any pleasure or satisfaction with it, it would be less effective to go backwards, so you go forward, always wanting more, trying to go above and beyond each last experience until there is no more to search for; until there are no more options to acquire a more powerful fantasy than the last. I was headed for an eternity of hell that started in the Devil's Dungeon. How appropriate.

Three days passed. I had had an epiphany in the shower. I realized I had fallen deep into another realm of sadism and murder. I had become a superior killing machine, like a robot with no empathy, no respect for human life, only programed to torture, destroy, to slaughter without any conscience. I realized at this point in my life, I would go to any length, any illegal, cruel, macabre or obscene extreme to equal and outdo all my former murder scenes that have taken place in each and every torture room. I had reached the outer limits of grizzly acts and there was no going back. I couldn't imagine what I would or could do that would be more macabre and repulsive than a decapitation.

Room 209 – Blue Pine Zoo

I call 209 The Zoo. Margie Tootle stands out in my mind. Margie was a sixty-five-year-old waitress about 5'2", an overweight and rugged looking grand mum type with salt & pepper hair in a big, bun and rosy, ball shaped rouge on her cheeks. Margie had stopped in for an overnight stay before driving back to New Hampshire. She said she saw the vacancy sign on the stately, Victorian mansion and was glad it was a guest house. Being curious, never having been inside such a magnificent structure, she decided to stop.

Margie had a wonderful smile, a gentle disposition and wore a familiar-smelling lady's cologne, a scent I recognized was sold by Avon. My mum wore that same fragrance called Cotillion for years. A scruffy-looking character with soiled slacks and a large brown case of products visited mum every few months to sell his Avon. I didn't like that salesman. He looked at me with dark evil eyes and a frown of disapproval of my presence. He also had a body odor. Yuck. I usually left mum alone with him and went outside or to my room if dad wasn't home.

I quietly sniffed Tootle's bold fragrance without her noticing. I hadn't smelled it since I was living with mum in New York. I also hadn't realized before this day that scent was a wicked trigger for me. Immediately, like a huge wave of turbulent memories came flooding over me in a tempest of strong, raging emotions. A bittersweet revelation, all too familiar of both good and bad, but mostly bad. The ugly man I was afraid of, the horrible religious lessons, the painful whippings from mum and images of victims of fatal car accidents, flashing in revolving sequence, swimming around my furious mind. I excused myself from Margie's interview to step outside for a breath of fresh, clean air to collect my composure and return directly to the tearoom with more sanity and poise.

In spite of her weight, Margie had a decent hourglass figure, was stacked up top and kind of sexy for her old age, with a brilliant sense of humor. I may have passed on permitting her accommodations and let her leave, I should have told her we just reserved the last room, but I didn't. I had to feed my pets.

Yesterday, Perry and Terry had started to fight with each other, so I had to feed them something soon. After our talk, where I learned about Margie's solitude life, heart problems and depressing family issues, I took the humble, dear, vulnerable, grand mum upstairs. Margie giggled and joked with me all the way up to the second floor, to the room I call the Blue Pine's Zoo. I opened the door of 209 and said, "Ladies first." In she walked, unaware of an unsafe situation. I closed the door behind me and turned on the light bulb above by pulling the string and all hell broke loose.

Margie took one look at the rats fighting in the small cage in front of her under the light, and simultaneously saw Pete, my Boa crawling across the floor and screeched so loud with freight and fear that she collapsed on the floor on top of Pete, hitting her head on the corner of the hard metal cage. She croaked right there and then with eyes and mouth wide open. I guessed it must have been her bad heart.

Unfortunately, I didn't have any time to slowly torture her, so I sat down on the chair beside the cage and watched my rats go crazy biting each other fiercely and savagely. I could tell they were about to eat each other, being over a week without food, so I opened the cage door and set the pair free. Perry and Terry were angry and hungry so I knew what was about to happen. I pulled my cigar from the inside pocket of my jacket, lit up and got comfortable to observe a theatrical, macabre performance by my starving pet rats that became instantly cannibalistic. I watched my rodents intently and took notes. Perry scurried straight for Margie's bulging eyes. He gobbled up those two succulent morsels, then went for her tongue and cheeks inside. Terry wasn't as fast or that lucky. The minute he approached Margie's dead body, Pete, my hungry boa grabbed Terry and coiled around him for his own dining pleasure. My Blue Pine Zoo put on a fabulous show for me that night. I was the only one who didn't get everything my way, but the sadistic entertainment had to suffice. I sat there as still and quietly as possible so not to distract or disturb the two enthusiastic performers. I stayed long enough to watch Perry chew his way into Margie's throat and disappeared out of sight. I had never seen a rat burrow into a corpse before. This was another first, so be it.

I got hungry watching the critters feast, so eventually I exited 209, locked the door and went to cook my dinner. I left the zoo creatures for the night to satisfy their hunger. I went to clean up in the morning and couldn't find Perry, but I was sure what had happened. He had burrowed through Margie and was somewhere down in her torso, I assumed, if he survived. He took a one-way path and maybe got lost inside big Margie Tootle. I put satiated Pete back into his enormous cage and stuffed Margie's corpse with Perry still inside, into an old WWII military, footlocker trunk so I could sanitize the floor.

Late that night, around 2:00 AM, I put the heavy trunk on a trolly with wheels and took it out the back door to the hearse. I drove the human cargo out to the dark, deserted dump. I backed in, dumped the trunk on a pile of garbage, and opened the lid to feed the dump's hungry rats. All in a night's work.

Quote: "What's past is prologue." ~ Shakespeare

AUTHOR'S WARNING FOR

'SATAN'S PLAYGROUND'

'Satan's Playground', Room 211 may be the darkest, most disturbing confession in this diary. Some readers may find it necessary to skip this segment of the 'Innkeeper' because it involves children. Some readers may find this graphically grotesque, heinous and/or obscene. Therefore, if obscenity and graphic, sexual literature offends you or is against your moral code, Room 211 must be avoided.

Do Not Enter.

Just for your information, there were at least 25 known male and female monstrous killers who preyed on children from the early 1900's to the new millennium. Some killers kept diaries describing in detail their deplorable criminal acts, like Kathleen Folbigg. One killer raped and murdered over 300 young girls and another tortured, raped and killed 138 young boys. All of these killers' sprees are documented in history's literature. (See the Glossary #64)

Satan's Playground tells about one child murder, so I included all of Andrew Webb's murders found in his journal. Andrew only detailed one child murder which is in the 'Innkeeper'.

If you choose to read Satan's Playground, read at your own risk with free will and open mind. 'Obscene' is in the eyes of the beholder. The author will take no responsibility for those who perceive this content to be obscene. The author chose to include this obscene confession found in Andrew's journal because the purpose of the 'Innkeeper' is to show and tell the readers everything that lurks deeply inside the minds of some serial killers. The thoughts, the desires and the evil crimes of Andrew Webb were written in Andrew Webb's journal. You have been warned.

Room 211 – Satan's Playground

I don't plan to use this room often. I shouldn't write anything in this journal about Room 211 because this confession will certainly disturb most everyone. But I do write about everything I think about, all the fantasies I desire, and everything I do. If those who are curious enough to read this, they must want to know what are the darkest desires that plague my sadistic, criminal mind and why and how I engaged in such unimaginable atrocities. I do confess, all the content in my journal is true and was documented by me only. I predict, if and when this journal is discovered, it will shine a new perspective on what goes on in the minds of some murderers who have thought about and committed the most immoral, forbidden, and obscene crimes known to man. I'm guilty as sin. I'm Andrew Webb.

I read child murders are rare, but my profile will encompass the traits and paraphilias of many types of killers. My sexually, sadistic desires range across the board because I'm also turned on by torturing and killing young boys for erotic, visual enjoyment and sexual gratification.

When I read about Marcel Proust's eccentricities and paraphilias, I thought I'd try a couple of his atrocities to see how it made me feel. I was moved by his starving rats scene, so I made a torture room especially for that. The Blue Pine Zoo. I'll write a tad more about the literary genius because I liked his style enough to experience it myself.

Proust lived across the street from a park where he could watch young boys play. He would order his assistant to go fetch a schoolboy and bring him upstairs. I won't go into detail about what happened in his apartment, but it's a good read if you're interested. My desires are somewhat different from Proust.

If I see a young boy that I'm attracted to playing in the school yard after classes adjourn for the day, or at the local park, I will stop and watch, maybe take photographs if I get close enough.

I abducted my first child prisoner, a nine-year-old, named Jeffrey, from the local park here in Briggstown. I bribed him into my car by telling him his mother hired me to pick him up to take him home. Jeffrey was a cute boy, a polite lad from a good home. I took notice of his respectful manners and I liked that. I was mild mannered and soft-spoken to him, but it took a little time to convince him to go with me because he was taught never to get in a car or go anywhere with a stranger. Finally, he acquiesced and got in the hearse and off we went back to the Blue Pine. I think he was fascinated as well as leery of the black, intimidating funeral car.

I coaxed Jeffrey inside with the story I had to pick up something for his mother. When he walked inside, I told him to help me get what his mum requested. It was in Room 211. I quickly locked the door behind me and told little Jeff I wanted to take a photo for his mum. After taking photos with his clothes on, I politely asked Jeffrey to remove his clothes, but he refused and tried to bolt out the door of 211. When he found the door was locked, he became arrogant at first but when I sat there calmy and poised and stared at him with a smirk, he began to cry, then to holler he wanted to go home. 211 was completely soundproofed for scenes like this. When he refused to undress, I resorted to more drastic measures. That's when I got impatient, angry and physically violent.

I had heard enough of all the crying, begging and screaming my sadistic nature could tolerate. I grabbed Jeffrey by his neck, pushed him down on the floor with my other hand and straddled his frail, sweet, pale virgin body. I covered his mouth and looked into his teared eyes and I said:

"Jeffrey, when I take my hand off your mouth and get up, you will be quiet and do exactly what I want you to do. Do you understand? Do I have your promise? Because if you don't, you will never see your mother again."

The boy nodded his head in agreement, so I got up and pulled him to his feet by clenching his thick, blonde, curly locks. I grabbed his arm and led him over to stand in front of the full-length mirror. There, I ordered him to remove his tan overalls and underwear. He did, but he was shaking and moving reluctantly. I took a few more photos. He was shivering uncontrollably, and tears were streaming down his flushed warm, rosy cheeks. I told him to slowly turn around so I could see every angle of his pert, small body. Unintentionally, his tiny pole started to rise, and he quickly covered it with both hands. I commanded him to take his hands away, to walk towards me and then close his eyes. Jeffrey started crying out loud again and pleading with me to let him go home. That was not on my agenda.

My next move was to fulfill my sexual fantasy with this nine-year old. To shut Jeffrey's mouth, I began to choke him, and he spontaneously regurgitated all over my hands and green suit jacket. That made me furious, so I continued to strangle him to death. I kept choaking him and telling him he was a bad boy long after he was dead, until blood started dripping from the corners of his eyes and down the side of his mouth. In no time, I was holding a dead child. It was the first time. He looked like a zombie from a Halloween movie. His face was gross; his body was completely limp and now I was ready to do what I had fantasized. I turned him over and propped his bum up in line with my trembling bollocks and held him by his hips, his body bent over forward. As challenging as it was, so small and tight, I sodomized Jeffrey until I was satiated and drained.

I dropped Jeffrey's abused body onto the floor and sat down with this journal to weigh my feelings about the scene I just committed. I had mixed emotions. I reviewed my sentiments and concluded something else about myself. Shagging the lad was a different sort of high, more of a power and control rape of sorts. Whether it's sadism, or torture, the strangling or mind game fantasies I play with my victims, each and every one adds a diverse feeling and diverse experience for my own sexual pleasures. However, it's with whoever, depending on my mood and the select human I choose; its necrophilia that is my end game and favorite paraphilia.

After soul-searching for an ample amount of time, I carried the boy to the dumping chute and dropped his corpse from Satan's Playground down the chute to the Devil's Dungeon.

During dinner that night, I imagined another devilish, fantasy delight. I didn't want to decapitate the little lad, no, no. I didn't care to execute more abuse to his little corpse. I had the bizarre notion to preserve him, to keep the boy with me indefinitely. I hadn't done that before.

Immediately, I joined the young corpse waiting for me in the basement. I removed Jeffrey's organs, stuffed plugs in all his orifices, hosed off the blood and vomit, then I embalmed Jeffrey with formaldehyde. I stuffed his body with Styrofoam, glued his eyelids down and lips together. I put his body in the cooler temporarily, so I had time to plan a course of action to proceed. I had done some research on the history of preserving a body when I worked in the morgue. The first documentation of embalming with formaldehyde dates back to 1899, I learned while doing research.

I became obsessed with wanting to preserve Jeffrey's body so it would last longer than using only formaldehyde embalming fluids. I experimented with wax, to create a liquid wax solution. It came out satisfactorily, so I was encouraged to go forward. I took Jeffrey out of the refrigerator, washed him with water and disinfectant before I lightly coated his entire body with my wax solution by both spraying his body and using a sponge. I had never tried this before and had never heard of it before. It was an idea out of my curious, creative mind. I wanted it to work, so I could keep Jeffrey in my cooler as long as possible. I called him 'My Prize Boy.' After the wax, I wrapped his entire corpse with a tough plastic material and put him directly back into the coldest, negative temperature refrigerator to freeze his corpse. That way, Jeffrey's body would be preserved for months before it started to decompose. During that time, I could visit him in the refrigerator. When the time comes when his corpse starts to decompose, I will cremate him, put him in a pretty urn and set it on my dresser for a keepsake. I want to remember Jeffrey. He was my finest specimen. He reminded me of me.

Three months have passed, now I'm back to my journal. My Prize Boy stayed in good shape for a few months. I visited the young lad twice a week to refresh my visuals and to stimulate and relive my fantasies. He was the only child I kidnapped. He was the only one out of three whom I became attached to. Other children were defiant and rude or cold and ill-mannered, so I didn't want to keep any of them, just a piece of clothing and a photo or two. I prefer adolescents.

Room 213 - Coffin Chaos

I used a female guest who I considered appropriate for 213. A lady about 5'6', with short brunette hair, a big bum, an average build, olive skin and a beautiful smile. Her name was Helena. Helena came through my door the day after this room was ready. The first thing I noticed was this woman's long, deep cleavage on her bum. She told me she taught school in Portland and would be visiting Bar Harbor to see her recently married daughter and new grandchild. I found out over tea and petit fours Helena was forty-one, and her family didn't know she was coming to visit. It was a surprise for her grandson's second birthday, so no one expected her, in fact, this was another perfect scenario; no one will miss her. Helena was tired, so she took a detour off her designated route, drove through Briggstown and stopped at the Blue Pine Guest Inn for an overnight stay before driving further to her destination. Her time of arrival in the early evening provided an opportunity for me and I took full advantage of it.

I had greeted the lovely lady at the door in my mid-thigh length, elegant, blue velvet smoking jacket, a maroon ascot tie cravat, my curved handle pipe and antique brass handle walking cane. My appearance presented that of a refined, wealthy gentleman which is effective with women and assures them they are safe and in good hands. I added more attractions this time to enhance my obvious charismatic and debonaire style. My British accent and attire assured Helena of class and safety and being confident with my entire production would surely convince her to check in. I knew women in the United States were fascinated and often persuaded by certain foreign accents. My British accent sounded sexy and worked with much success.

My classical attire is also in color coordination with the Victorian era motif of my tearoom salon. As I mentioned earlier, my intention for the Blue Pine's image and reputation is that of the most fashionable, Victorian ambiance hosted by a chivalrous, honorable gentleman. The flip side of this assumed high social status I portray is the other half of my dark, double life. I will describe my first experience in the Room 213 with the dialog that transpired between Helena and me.

"Helena, my dear, if you don't care for another tad of tea, would you care for a sip of bourbon, brandy or cognac for your nightcap this evening?"

"I thought you'd never ask, young man. I've had my eye on your crystal brandy snifters collection and that handsome pipe snifter. Where were you fortunate enough to find that precious piece? I would love to enjoy a brandy tonight before I retire. Thank you for your generous hospitality."

"Wonderful, Miss Helena, I believe I will join you this evening for a brandy. There is nothing better to warm the body and soul on such a chilly night. Has anyone ever told you, you have beautiful, raven hair. It's absolutely divine."

I admit, I'm generous with compliments with some of the ladies. Frequently I will flirt, it's another one of my con techniques, because I never have the intention to be romantic with any of my guests though they usually assume I'm after sex when I flirt. Most definitely, my sexual desires are post-mortem with some of them, but never when they're breathing.

"I'm delighted to have spent this time with you, Mr. Webb. I would like to go to my room now. I'm feeling sleepy so the bed is going to feel good tonight. Once again, thank you for your divine hospitality and that delicious apple brandy. You surely know how to impress a lady."

"Certainly, my dear. I will escort you up to your room on the second floor. I think you will be delighted with your accommodation. Once you're settled in, if there is anything at all I can do to make your visit better, don't hesitate to push the button on the inside of your door which rings a bell at the front desk and in my private quarters. An English breakfast of crumpets and café will be available tomorrow morning between 7:00 AM and 9:00 AM. Here you are, ma'am."

I always make my guests feel comfortable and secure in the beginning before I trap them in my web of deceit.

"Thank you very much for your grand hospitality, Mr. Webb. I believe I've already thanked you. I suppose I'm feeling a bit tipsy from that luscious brandy."

"Helena, you may call me, Andrew."

"Well, yes, yes, thank you, Andrew. I was about to call you, Sir Andrew. You surely look like an English nobleman. I'm thoroughly impressed with the elegance, charm and décor here at the Blue Pine. I'm sure I will enjoy my stay."

"Here we are, Helena, darling. Here's your room. Anything else for you this evening, ma'am? Ladies, first." I always escort my guests to their 'doom room' with my warm, pleasant protocol. I unlocked the door and told Helena to enter before me. I didn't turn on a light until we were both inside the room with the door closed behind me. I flicked on the blue lighting, just enough illumination to show the warm parlor part of the room. It had a vintage Victorian sofa covered in a soft, coral velvet sitting alone against the wall.

"Andrew, what is this? Is this my room? There's no bed. Where is my room? Where have you taken me! I don't like this room, Andrew."

"Relax dear, this is only part of your surprise."

I took Helena by her elbow and led her through the next door. This section of the room was a dark crypt with its creepy, glossy caskets and two cracked tombstones. Helena went into a terrifying rage, screaming loudly.

"What is this horrible place? Why have you taken me here, Andrew!"

"Relax, my dear. Let me show you around."

"You're crazy, get me out of here. Get me out of here right now!"

Helena turned around and raced for the door knocking into me. I grabbed her from behind by the neck and squeezed with enough pressure to make her slow down and feel lightheaded so I could lead her over to the attractive, pine coffin with peach silk-lined interior I had brought up from the display room downstairs. It was the only coffin amongst the caskets. Helena was in a state of shock and confusion. I forced her to sit on the seat attached to a winch I had erected in 213 to be able to hoist someone up into the coffin. I instructed her to step into the coffin, but she started screaming obscenities at me instead. It appeared Helena was going to give me a hard time. Without another word, I lowered the seat into the coffin carefully and yanked the seat out from under her bum. She plopped down into the coffin still swearing at me and tried frantically to get up and out of it. I wasn't going to ruin my new creation or my plan, so I knocked her in the head with the brass crown handle of my walking stick. That laid her down but not unconscious.

"Think of this resting place as therapy, Helena. Coffin therapy. When I close the lid, don't fight it, close your eyes for you will be in utter peace and tranquility. There's nothing else in the world like it and.."

"Don't you dare close that lid, Andrew, you get me out of this horrible thing before I lose my temper! I bet your neighbors will hear me yelling and call for the police, so help me up out of here!"

"My dear lady, this room is insulated and soundproofed. I assure you; no one will hear you yelling. Do yourself a favor and lay still and quiet."

As I slowly closed the heavy lid, Helena let out a thunderous and shrieking scream the likes I had only heard in a horror movie. I couldn't help to be startled for a second then I started laughing at her misery. I had installed a hose for air inside the coffin near the head. I told Helena to put the hose in her mouth if she needed more air. The lid was down, and my ungrateful guest started feverishly kicking and banging the lid and sides of the antique, wooden box. I let her scream and get it out of her system thinking the brandy would eventually put her to sleep because I had put a tad of heroin in her cocktail. I knew she wasn't able to get out and would be passed out soon.

Meanwhile, I went downstairs for another brandy and my pipe. Brandy and a pipe go together like peanut butter and jelly. I picked up smoking this pipe when I bought the Blue Pine. It was suited for my charming Victorian décor and outfit.

I prefer a vanilla-flavored tobacco because it smells delightful and somewhat calming to most guests in my tearoom. After my brandy and a smoke, I returned to room 213 to check on my guest doing her coffin therapy. I raised the lid of the coffin quickly and Helena sat straight up like a corpse with rigor mortis with a look of madness on her red, sweaty face and she tried to climb out again, hysterically screaming and swearing vulgarity at me, using the most profane language I've only heard from drunk sailors in a seaside barroom. I struck her knuckles brutally with the handle of my trusty walking stick which knocked her back down into the cozy, sinister container. I knew she could hear me so I talked to her.

"Helena, Helena, dear one. This comfy accommodation is especially for you, my dear. Aren't you enjoying your therapy?"

"No, Andrew Webb, you will not get away with this, so let me out of this disgusting piece of shit! I swear I'll kill you!" I had to slam her hands again.

"Helena, (tisk, tisk), such language, from a lady. I should wash your dirty mouth out with turpentine. I thought you were a lady, Helena, but you're no different from the rest of the whores. For your information and my pleasure, we are going to play a little game. My favorite game. It's called, The Crypt Keeper."

"Never you mind about my language or any damn game, you son of a bitch. Let me out of here!"

Her nasty, frightened language was fun and stimulating for me because I liked being the boogie man scaring the hell out of her. The power and control gives me a rush. It gets my engine revved up, puts my psychopathic, criminal mind in gear and activates my sexual arousal. When my adrenaline rush goes on overdrive, I'm on a super high ready for intense action and I can't stop until I'm satisfied.

I didn't let Helena say another word. I immediately stuffed my sorry guest's mouth with a handful of soil I had sitting in a pale under the coffin. She gasped and choked and tried to spit it out in vain, but I kept replacing the soil, shoving, and packing it into her open mouth and nostrils, like I had invented another way to bury someone alive. She kept flailing her arms about trying to knock the soil out of my hands, so it took a while longer than I had expected. It made a dreadful mess inside that beautiful coffin which I had lined myself. A mixture of her spit and dirt plus her stinky sweat and body fluids were nauseating. I had anchored the coffin securely onto a heavy catafalque to hold a possible five-hundred pounds of weight, knowing I'd be adding my weight by jumping into one of them to sexually assault my victim. She choked and spewed dirt and spit all over and some was splattered on my chin and jacket until she gagged and then choked to death serenading me with the familiar death rattle.

The second phase of my pleasure, I brutally molested and raped Helena's dead body. I bit her inner thigh so hard I almost took out a clump of fatty flesh off her smooth leg into my mouth. My mouth was oozing with plasma; blood mixed with my saliva and there were bits of her tender white skin between my teeth. That was the first for me. Not biting an inner thigh, but the first time I got a taste of cannibalism. I licked my lips, sucked her skin off my teeth, then swallowed her flesh. It tasted somewhat like pork, and not like any other meat I've tasted. I may have eaten the chunk I almost bit off, but I already had my mind on something else before dinner and for dinner. That was a mere appetizer. It was a little strange, even for me, but I was certain things would get better later.

After Helena had passed, I had my erotic fulfillment in a mega orgasm. I was so excited shagging her violently my release was so powerful I collapsed and fell onto Helena's dead body. After I recovered, I sat up and removed her heart-shaped gold necklace for a souvenir and sat there on her torso, staring at her dirty, ugly face full of soil, drool and puke. It was right then I decided to leave her corpse in the coffin to rot. That's what the foul-mouthed whore deserved. I slid down the side of the coffin, took a deep breath and sat on the floor to regain my strength. In a few minutes, I went to the kitchen to get a bedtime snack. I always get hungry after a rough, enthusiastic shag.

Room 215 – 'Bettie Page' Dive

In Room 215, I planned to order a female guest to do an erotic striptease and other sexual activities to herself while I observe and take photos. I would like her to think I'm a bold, demanding, kinky fellow but she will know something isn't right. This scene will serve as a prelude to a different sort of sexual gratification for me. The erotic photos will remind me of the specific scene so I can relive it when I don't have a new prospect for a while or during a cooling off period.

It's been precisely six months since I've preyed on another victim. I learned how and when to stay low, under the cops' radar and that takes discipline on my part. During the last six months, I have solely relied on my vast collection of photographs and souvenirs to masturbate with. I have purposely avoided hunting and passed up two lovelies that would have been perfect, but too risky.

Yesterday, I couldn't resist Isabel. She resembled Bettie Page with her jet black, straight, shoulder length hair, same style of Bettie's trademark bangs, pretty blue eyes and a wide, red lipstick smile. I didn't have to ponder what guest room to take this beauty to, there was no mistake Room 215 was Isabel's destination because of the festive, feminine décor and photograph studio with a small stage and chrome dancing pole. I wanted some sexy entertainment.

I was excited when Isabel walked through my door requesting overnight accommodation. I couldn't believe my eyes and since I had patiently waited over six months, I wasn't going to wait another day. I captivated her with my British accent, flirtatious advances, and gentleman's etiquette on steroids to make sure I won her affection, at the least, her attention. We talked over two glasses of my best Pinot Grigio, and I slipped a little something in her first glass. I wanted to make sure this tart didn't change her mind. I learned she was a barmaid in a nightclub in Atlanta during their

November through April season but came to Maine to get a job in a bar or restaurant for the summer months here. She told me she was twenty-two, broke up with her boyfriend before leaving Georgia and her parents had died in a fatal car accident three years ago. No one knew where she had gone for the summer. My mouth started watering with delight on hearing what a great opportunity this would be. I was restless to get her up to Room 215, so I calmed down with two glasses of wine with her. I was past due needing a new fantasy and presto, here she appeared. Lucky me. I put on my charm and whisked Isabel straight up to my special, Bettie Page Salon in 215. This Friday night would be a night to remember. I unlocked the door and told Isabel to go on in. The red spotlights went on with a flip of the switch while I locked the door behind me. Isabel stopped dead in her tracks, speechless for a moment and gasped, not in fright, but in amazement. She collected herself and I could see the way she looked from left to right, and right to left that she was confused as to her surroundings. Her spiked wine had already taken effect, so I spoke up.

"My dear Isabel, is this a nice surprise for you? I thought you might like what I've created for my guests amusement which is always my pleasure."

"Mr. Webb, what is this? Why did you bring me here. I thought I was going to my room for the night, but there's no bed here. Why am I here? I want to go to bed, I'm feeling rather tipsy and lightheaded. It's been a long day and an enjoyable evening."

"But this is your room, dear Isabel, your special room for the night, so make yourself comfortable on this velvet couch first and I'll tell you what we're going to do. Yes, have a seat right here and I'll get us another drink."

"No, no thank you, Mr. Webb, I just want to go to my room and get some sleep."

"Come on my dear, this won't hurt you. A little nightcap before bedtime will help you sleep."

Saying that, I poured Isabel another cold glass of wine. At that point, my Dr. Jekyll demeanor turned about face to Mr. Hyde.

My dual personality reversed to my cruel, violent self. This is what happens when I unleash the evil urges inside me, so I can carry out my sinful cravings.

"Isabel, my dear, I want you to get onto that stage, right there under the red spotlight and do a sexy strip tease slowly for me."

The look of anguish and fear flooded Isabel's face as she stood up, screaming and ran towards the door. I grabbed her arm tightly and squeezed it roughly as she tried to get past me.

"No, dear, you're not going anywhere, Isabel. I wasn't asking you to do a strip tease, I was commanding you to do a strip tease. You will do as I say, so get up there and start taking off your clothes or I will rip them off you. I am going to take photographs of you, so do a good job. Entertain me, act like a model for me so I can get some good shots of you. Pretend you're Bettie Page and pose the way she would if she was here. Do you understand? This is not a joke, Isabel."

"No, Andrew, this is crazy shit, I'm not going to do a strip, I want to leave this mad house, so I'm going to go now!"

"No dear, I don't have to let you go and I'm not going to, so do the strip tease, or suffer the consequences."

Isabel knew I meant business. When I lose my patience and get angry when my select guest doesn't obey me immediately, I have the look of the devil in my stare. Isabel abruptly pulled away from me and gave me a stare back, if looks could kill. She reluctantly meandered towards the stage swaying and tripping on her own feet, so I had to laugh. She turned and looked at me like a female devil incarnate and started slowly removing her clothes, never taking her evil eyes off mine. Guess I met my match, such a challenge I will delight in. Isabel grabbed the chrome pole I had installed into the one step up stage. I'm a shutter nutter of sorts, so I took numerous photographs of Isabel in all positions of her sloppy strip tease show with my Kodak Instamatic, and a few minutes of her in supposed, sexy action with my 16mm cinecamera mum bought me for Christmas several years ago. I've been in the habit of photographing all my doomed guests antemortem and postmortem since I've lived alone. I have an extensive collection in the back of my journal.

Isabel finally fell down on the stage and didn't try to get up, faking a pass out that aggravated me more. I took a few more shots of her helpless, drugged body lying in an unattractive, half nude heap, hanging half on and off the stage. When I had satisfied my need for snapping photographs, it was time to change the pace to have my way. First, I had some words to lay on the helpless sket. I said.

"Isabel, you worthless sket. Stop playing games with me, you useless crumpet! You don't fool me in the slightest. You're a disgrace of a stripper and an insult to Bettie Page, so I hereby warn you, you will not like where this evening goes."

I took the razor blade I kept on top of the door and cut off her bra and soiled, drenched knickers, more proof I scared the life out of her. I admit, that was an ego trip. I dragged her floppy, disgusting body over to the loveseat couch and bent her face down into the cushion and torso over the arm with her wet snatch staring at me. This lassie didn't even trim her hair. Ugh.

Isabel was still alive, just barely conscious and that did nothing to arouse me, so it was time to bump her off to get my jollies. I guzzled down my glass of wine and slit her throat from ear to ear with the razor, then the gore unfolded. It took several swipes of my dull razor and in that process, I gouged her carotid artery which sent spurting streams of blood pumping out of Isabel's neck in a horrific fashion. My lacy cuff didn't avoid the blood pulses, neither did the floor and velvet couch. I became livid and I would have to get rid of the couch and mop that floor. I pulled an extra tie out of my back pocket and wrapped it around Isabel's neck to restrain the blood and finish strangling her.

I compartmentalized visuals of that bloody disaster and stayed focus with my desire to bonk the dead bitch, but first I needed to wank my willie to overcome the messy scene and to distract me from looking at her hairy, revolting muff. Just before I tossed it off, I grabbed both sides of her hips, closed my eyes and rammed my tool into the cleavage of her big bum. On the second stroke, I lost it all over her back. I took my tool in hand and plummeted down on the blood-soaked couch, exhausted with anxiety and pleasure from one of the ugliest scenes I'd had recently since the decapitation. Unfortunately, I had to get out of my fabulous Bettie Page salon because the bloody disarray was too much for me to deal with then.

I was in no mood to clean up the mess that night, so I left Isabel's nude corpse hanging over the arm of the couch, stuffed my stinky wet willie back in my pants and headed for the kitchen. I always work up a big appetite after a murder scene and Isabel's was more frustrating, so I'm extra hungry. I have left over cheese-stuffed pasta shells in the refrigerator with lots of marinara gravy and Italian garlic bread. That will hit the spot tonight.

Tomorrow, after coffee and a toasted English muffin, I will prepare to drag Isabel to the dump chute and drop her body down to the basement, if she will fit through the opening. I'll wash down 215, disinfect it and remove the upholstery from the couch so I can destroy it with her corpse. Late tomorrow night, Gerry or Joe will take the frame of the couch to the dump in the hearse. That was the intention, but that's not exactly what ultimately happened.

Joe drove to the dump late the following night, but two other people were there sitting on the hood of their truck drinking beer, so he drove the couch frame back to the Blue Pine. I scolded him for bringing it back because those lads at the dump wouldn't have thought it strange to dump a couch frame.

I retrieved surgical metals from Isabel's ashes remembering she had told me the story about her metal hip replacement by a Dr. Austin T. Moore many years ago at Columbia Hospital in South Carolina. Supposedly, her Dr. Moore was a famous giant of orthopaedic surgery for performing the first metal hip replacement in 1940.

I completed Isabel's cremation process by pulverizing all bone fragments in the cremulator. I had taken the surgical metals out of her ashes for a keepsake since they were implanted by a famous surgeon. After pulverizing the worthless barmaid, I threw the couch frame into the oven with the rest of the trash from 215. I had named Room 215 the Bettie Page Dive after meeting Isabel. Trash to trash.

Room 217 – Victorian Brothel

The first time, I initiated Room 217, was with a woman named Ginger. I was so disappointed in her performance, I killed her and it's not worth writing about. My second use of 217, I entertained a couple of ladies or better said, they entertained me. I kept Alice in the first chamber tied spread eagle to the poster bed and gagged and the other female guest, Toni, who had stayed over the night before was blindfolded and tied to one of the end posters. I had thought it would be double pleasure for me to hear how each woman reacted to hearing the other woman get brutalized and raped. This scene was another one of my sadistic experiments. I was satisfied with the results, so I will write a detailed experience into the journal about the scene memorable scene in 217 with Alice and Toni. This happened last week. This went well.

I invited my new guest Alice into my tearoom one Thursday afternoon for an interview and cocktail. She said she didn't drink alcohol, because she was eighteen. I didn't push it. I served her a cold Coca Cola soda with a little help from my stash of Mickey Finns. I hadn't tried it in a soda without liquor, but it did the job, nevertheless.

Alice was a pretty, petite, young teenager, about 5' tall with beautiful blonde curly hair, indigo blue eyes, fair skin and weighing no more than one-hundred pounds. She said she was eighteen, but she didn't look a day older than fifteen. Being young and innocent to drugs, alcohol, and the dangers of life, Alice was an easy mark. With a few minutes of our conversation, she was so weary, I took her to the second floor in my private elevator and straight into 217 which is near the elevator. She was putty in my hands. There was no resistance to tie her wrists up to the bed posts and strip off her slacks and knickers. I didn't need a gag for her mouth because she passed out completely before I finished the bondage. I stared intently at that thing between her leg because it was mostly bald with a few yellow hairs, so much better than those hairy things. I tried futilely to get a boner, knowing it was going to be a waste of time, but time was on my side. I loosened her wrist restraints and left her in the bedroom chamber for the night, hoping another young girl looking for a waitress's position in this area, would come to the Blue Pine. There was a good chance because it was the weekend.

Early, the next morning, I checked on Alice. She was half conscious and delirious asking where she was. I was thrilled later that day when Toni popped in, but I wasn't sure at first if she'd be a good fit for my new fantasy. I had to weigh the odds and not take a big risk. I had never dealt with two guests at the same time. Toni's interview seemed good except for the fact her brother lived in Kittery, Maine and he knew she was headed to Briggstown before Bar Harbor. My needs were desperate and careless that night, so I decided to take a big risk and bring the new guest into my scheme because she had the perfect appearance. Toni was a dark-olive skin, athletic, Latin female, thirty-five, with extremely short black hair in a ducktail hairstyle and Pistachio green eyes. She was a handsome, manly-looking woman wearing a suit jacket and tie if you like that, but not my type. Alice was my type. Alice was perfect. I hadn't run across Alice's sort since I had moved from southern Maine, so she was a gift indeed.

Toni gladly accepted my hospitality. She drank the last half-fifth of my costly bourbon and was waiting to be offered more, but I cut her off. I excused myself for a five-minute check up on Alice tied up in the bondage chamber. I turned on a soft light and assured her I was coming right back. I was pleasantly surprised she didn't scream or cry; maybe too much in shock.

I went downstairs to get Toni and escort her up to Room 217. She was intoxicated but still able to walk and talk without a problem. I told her I had met someone I wanted her to meet before she retired to her room. I wasn't wearing my Victorian best, only a dapper sports coat, but I took it off and flung it onto a chair as we left the tearoom parlor. Toni, energetic and full of curiosity followed me up the stairway to the second floor. I opened the door, ushered Toni inside and simultaneously locked the door behind me. She stopped dead in her tracks and uttered a loud gasp.

"What is this weird dark room about, Mr. Webb? It looks like a whorehouse in here. What gives with that? Is this a joke? Seriously, it looks like a cheap brothel with the red lights and all. Thought you wanted me to meet someone?" I said to her.

"You'll see. You're going to like the surprise that's waiting for you."

I took Toni's arm and guided her over to the scarlet red curtain of the second chamber, slid it open and gently pushed Toni inside.

"Holy shit, Webb, this is a damn dungeon! Why did you bring me here? I'm not into this sick shit, so I'm going to leave."

Toni turned around and walked right into me. Stunned and wild-eyed, she excused herself and stepped aside, but I grabbed both of her sinewy arms and walked her backwards six long steps straight into the wall rack. She tried to pull away and almost succeeded, but the liquor had dulled her strength and reasoning just enough for me to force her wrists into the ropes hanging from the bondage rack. That was a close call and could have been a problem, but my determination exceeded her limited strength. I talked to Toni nicely to calm her down, but that didn't work. She vehemently swore at me, spit at me and threatened me, saying I had made a big mistake by kidnapping her because her father was in the FBI and I would pay dearly. I didn't believe a word of her ruse, so I continued.

"I'm sorry you feel that way, Toni. Thank you for the warning. I will definitely take heed."

I bound her waist with rope and secured her ankles into the rack below.

"When I get out of here, I'm going to kill you Webb unless you set me free now. Set me free and I'll leave quietly and forget this ever happened. I'll forget I ever met you!"

"Not a chance my dear. You will never leave the Blue Pine now. You're too much of a liability sweetheart, you will never see the light of day again."

With Toni screaming obscenities and hostile threats at me, I smacked a ball gag in her mouth and left her there to stew. I went in to see my pretty little Alice to stir things up another notch. Alice was awake. I took a rag and wiped the saliva off her cheeks and chin.

She was such a docile delight, it was too bad Toni was being a fool. The three of us could have had a wicked good time. Such a shame.

"There, that looks better Alice. How are you doing today, honey? I see you have wet yourself. I loved those black satin sheets I bought in New York. I'll let that mistake slide if you are a good girl."

"Please let me go, Mr. Webb. I'm begging you to let me go."

"No, my sweet, not now." I said affectionately. I had to fake being compassionate when it was necessary. Toni didn't stop cursing with threats.

"Who's on the other side of the wall, Mr. Webb? Who is yelling so loud?"

"That's Toni, Alice. I'll introduce you soon."

I didn't expect what Alice did next.

"Toni! Toni! Can you hear me! Toni, please, please come and get me out of here!"

Furthermore, I was not expecting Toni's response. I was amused by their back and forth screaming to each other, so I let it go on for a short time.

"Who the hell are you? I'm all tied up and can't help myself! What's your name?"

"I'm Alice, Toni! I'm tied up, too, and I want to get out of this hell hole. What is he going to do with us?"

"Ditto, Alice. I want to get out of here, too! I don't know, but it won't be good. Where is the monster?"

"He's here on the other side of the wall. He's sitting on a chair writing something. He's smiling, can you believe this, he's got a demented looking smile!"

"Writing something? What the hell! What is going on here? Is he some kind of reporter or cop or something? What are we both doing here?"

"I thought I came here to rent a room, Toni?"

All of a sudden, the conversation between my two scared prisoners stopped. I had already written down most of their frightful banter so I wouldn't forget it. It had come to the time for the tension and excitement in 217 to escalate. I chose to start with Alice. My once sweet 'Alice in Wonderland'. She remined me of a quote from 'Alice in Wonderland' that I recite aloud to myself when I'm challenged with risk or fear.

"Have I gone mad? I'm afraid so. You're entirely bonkers. But I'll tell you a secret. All the best people are." ~ Lewis Carroll.

Another quote I remember from 'Alice in Wonderland' by Lewis Carroll applies to me as well.

"Imagination is the only weapon in the war on reality."

After reciting those quotes, I often think of myself as the Mad Hatter, especially when I wear my top hat. There I go, getting distracted. Back to writing about my experience in 217.

As much as I hadn't planned to ruin Alice's pretty face and body, I couldn't help myself. The sadistic devil came out in me in a flurry of uncontrollable insanity. Inflicting pain, fear and agony is my foreplay. Watching someone suffer, enduring intense pain is my prelude to sex. I get turned on hurting someone but shagging a corpse... Humm. Sweet, young Alice looked so nice laying there tied to the bed, but I had to shake things up. I stared into Alice's beautiful eyes for two seconds and said, lassie, I'm sorry, but this is going to hurt. Then, I unleashed my evil desires and started beating her delicate, flawless flesh with a bamboo cane. I administered dozens of harsh lashes all over her breasts, stomach, muff and thighs. I mutilated her nipples and clitoris with my pocketknife and extracted one of her indigo blue eyes to keep for a souvenir. That poor little girl screamed, cried, and shrieked louder than I had ever heard before. It sounded so good and felt so damn good to me.

At the same time, Toni in the next chamber was shouting at the top of her lungs and thrashing around violently trying to get loose. I worked on Alice's body until my right shoulder was sore. Then I got up on the bed, straddled her bleeding, welted torso and slowly strangled her soft white neck with my strong fingers until she stopped gasping and gurgling. I put Alice out of all her misery with my tie routine, tucked in my back pocket.

Toni's deafening screams had intensified with fear to such a volume, I began to worry if 217 had enough soundproof for this unexpected scene. I left Alice's dead body temporarily and walked around the wall to enjoy Toni's fear and desperation. That butch, young lady heard thirty minutes of a horrific preview of what to expect for herself, so when she saw me, her threats turned to begging. Talk about me being a Jekyll and Hyde, this girl did a 360. I sat down on the chair positioned next to the wall rack, took my notepad out from under the cushion and began to document every word, everything that went down. I took a break from writing to start torturing Toni, knowing I was excited to get back to Alice while her tender body was still appealing to me. Toni begged, cried and pleaded with me but I didn't feel an ounce of pity for her and of course no remorse for Alice. In the meantime, I had at least an hour or two before Alice became cold and rigor mortis set in, though I knew I couldn't wait that long.

I had plenty more of foreplay fun with my other wiry, terrified victim to prolong her suffering. I looked at her with disdain, as a living piece of helpless prey and I was the anxious predator.

I know I'm considered mentally ill by society's laws and standards, but I have no control. I inflicted maximum pain on Toni by brutally beating about her head and face with the same cane used on Alice. I cut her clothes off from top to bottom with sharp scissors I had left on top of the rack and laughed heartily at her as I savagely ripped her rags down off her shaking body. When I released her restraints, her body fell down off the rack onto the carpeted floor. I kicked and stomped on her knockers and muff so hard until streams of blood ran down her torso and thighs. I trampled her anguished face until it was unrecognizable, and several teeth had fallen out. I was compelled to talk to her while I was squashing her bazooms and muff with my heavy boots.

"By the look of you when I first saw you tonight, I could tell by the way looked you don't like men, do you? You're a faggot, a dyke. I hate dykes! Take this cunt; it will be my ultimate pleasure to get rid of you! The world would be a lot better off without you damned dykes!"

That freak was so full of blood and bruises that there wasn't much skin that hadn't been abused into deep shades of red and blue. After I started getting aroused from inflicting excruciating pain, I proceeded to sexually assault the lesbo bitch. Shagging her wasn't a sexual act for me, it was an act of violence. For half an hour, I repeatedly shagged Toni's mouth, her bum and muff but held my release for pretty Alice who was patiently and quietly waiting for me on the other side of the wall.

I ended Toni's disgusting, pathetic screams with a quick, hard kick to her temple with the pointed toe of my boot. Then I rushed back to Alice to continue building up to the crescendo. Pretty, warm, dead Alice received all my pent-up hostility and hate of Toni. I ejaculated my heavy load all over her pretty face and into her empty eye socket. I experienced one of the most intense orgasms I'd ever had. I put Alice's right eyeball in a small mason's jar full of formaldehyde and labeled it Alice. It is sitting on top of the tall bureau in my private suite. It's an excellent keepsake to remind me of the most exceptional night I've ever experienced dominating and punishing two females. I think that was a once in a lifetime scene for me.

The next day, I cleaned up the mess and smell I had abandoned in 217 the night before. I moved two useless, cold, stiff bodies over to the garbage chute, then had another idea. Rigor Mortis had taken its course, so I had to break their stiffened joints with a sludge hammer to stuff their bodies into large garbage bags. I thoroughly cleaned the room with antiseptic, before taking a break to get some dinner, a strong drink and smoke my pipe. I drank too much that stunning night listening to music to sooth my soul and waited until after midnight to finish the job. I loaded the cumbersome bags into the boot of Toni's 1951 Chevy and took my passengers fifteen minutes away into a neighborhood town and disposed of both cadavers on a dark, lakeside road. On the way home, I thought to myself, the next time, I want to use 217, I'll execute a shower scene to terrorize my guest. That'll be new for me, too. Might be fun stabbing a woman to death in the shower. I wondered if any murderers had done a shower scene yet?

Room 219 – Necktie Party

An immature, egotistical and critical bloke came to the Blue Pine seeking accommodations for one night. His name was James. He drank my wine and made fun of my Victorian outfit. He asked if I was aware New Year's Eve was over? Then he criticized my lovely, tearoom décor saying it was too feminine for male guests. I bit my tongue, knowing I would have the last word that day. I let him go on and on about how great a chef he was going to be and that he would turn the big island on its heels with his amazing seafood cuisine recipes. I listened to him brag about every dish including his soon to be famous, Lobster Fra Diablo, then I told him it was time to show him to his room. I couldn't wait any longer to get a noose around his skinny, miserable neck. I had picked out the perfect name for him, so I started calling him Jesse James on the way upstairs. My anger had been festering during his interview in the parlor, so by the time we arrived at the door of 219, revenge was the only thought I pondered. There wasn't a better suited room for this character than 219.

I pushed the door open with an abrupt, forceful thrust and stood back so James could enter before me, as usual, my victim always enters a room first. I was ecstatic I had set the room up with a western motif, never knowing if Room 219 would be the ideal setting for a guest. But this setting seemed perfect for the way I felt about James.

I flipped on the light switch and vola, you would have thought you had traveled back in time to a town in the old, old west. I had supplied 219 with a few pieces of western gear including a gun in a holster (unloaded) for the guest and a hat and gun in a holster for me. In my mind, Jesse James was an outlaw, and I was the sheriff with a lynching mob. Immediately, I put on my holster while James was curiously looking around. He criticized my choice of décor, said he could have done a better job with his eyes closed, then asked why he was taken to that room where there was no bed instead of the room for his overnight accommodations. I told him we were going to play a game before I took him to his room. I told James to play along and strap on the gun, put on the hat and I would explain. He reluctantly obliged, and I told him this.

"Pretend you were Jesse James, the outlaw, bank and train robber, the wild west's most legendary outlaw, until you got caught by the sheriff and his posse. I will role-play the sheriff, so call me, Sheriff Webb. Come on, be a good sport and let's have some fun tonight."

He looked at me with eyes that could kill and yelled,

"You're mad! You're crazy! What kind of game is this? What are you doing, man? Are these guns loaded? You're a madman, Webb! I'm leaving to find a different motel. You can keep your weird guest house, games, guns and everything because this is insane!" I said to him.

"Jesse James, you won't be going anywhere except up on that scaffold."

I drew my gun on him and at the same time James drew his gun and started shooting at me. Shooting blanks at me. I laughed and bellowed until tears came to my eyes. That play by James made my night worth the wait already.

"You didn't think I was stupid enough to give you a gun with live rounds did you? You are more ignorant than I originally thought, James. You might as well drop your gun and start walking. Start walking up the stairs to the top of that scaffold. This isn't a choice, Jesse James, it's an order."

I drew my gun and pointed it at him and told him to move it.

"You've got to be kidding, Webb. I'm not going anywhere except out of this hell hole, so move aside because I'm leaving here and stop calling me Jesse James!"

I walked over to him and cocked the trigger, showing him my gun was loaded.

"For the last time, go up on that scaffold! Now!"

A sweat broke out on James's forehead, and he started to tremble so much that he couldn't yell anymore, only nervous blubbering dribbled off his former, belligerent tongue. I had deflated his ego, and he saw his fate was literally looming overhead. My next victim, James, was headed for a grizzly, horrific death. I couldn't stop laughing at him and kept poking my gun into his back all the way up to the top of the scaffold. This western parody was more fun than I had anticipated. This impudent fool deserved everything he had coming to him and I was going to have a fun night.

On the top of the scaffold, I secured James's wrists behind him in the metal handcuffs I had waiting on the railing, then led him over to stand on the trapdoor. I had designed this scaffold to be six feet off the floor to accommodate most men. James was five feet, eight inches tall, so that would work for him. My poor, insolent chef had urinated all over himself and his shirt had become soaked with sweat against his back and chest. His lack of communication told me he knew he was going to die and there was nothing he could do about it. I didn't expect a man like him to react with dignity facing such a cruel and violent method of death. His sublime resignation to his situation didn't faze me one bit, it just took a little pleasure out of my ultimate thrill. This murder was exciting enough. I had no regrets.

The blue spotlight shown directly down on the top of James's red-hair crew cut. He bent his head back to look up at the light, closed his eyes and started reciting the Lord's prayer. I put the noose over his head, around his neck, tightened the hangman's knot and placed it just ahead of his left ear and below his left lower jaw, like I saw in the westerns. I could become fond of this, especially for men I didn't like. In my mind, hanging wasn't for my female guests. Several other rooms were kept specifically for women.

The time for reckoning arrived and I was in no hurry to end his life before he suffered more emotionally. I went down the stairs off the scaffold and sat on the chair I provided for myself and lit up my pipe so I could embellish James's terror and get fully engulfed in his pain and agony. I wasn't into men, so I wouldn't be looking forward to shagging the lad after I killed him, but I was getting a thrill to watch and listen to him struggle to get loose and suffer with dreaded fear. He uttered sounds I've never heard from a man before. Sounded like a cross between whining and wincing. My exhilaration and satisfaction and on this day would depend solely on my sadistic desires. I gave in to masturbation sitting there looking up at my helpless, defenseless, scared to death prisoner. James's pain and fear was so intense, so awesome, I thought I should give it a try. I had a one-man audience. It worked. Whew, what a blast to be an executioner. I put willie back in my pants, stood up and walked over to the lever. I took one last look at Jessie James's shameful face and pulled the lever down firmly. It made a deafening thud; the trap door fell down and James fell through bouncing and swaying to and fro kicking his legs back and forth for a minute. That whole scene ignited, stimulated and thoroughly satisfied my sexual sadism needs with a powerful and noisy climax of James's gurgling and choaking. Maybe I was born too late? I might have like living in the Wild West.

I had never witnessed a hanging in person before, so I didn't know exactly how it would play out. James's execution went brilliantly well. His body dangled on the noose a mere few inches off the floor for a few minutes until his body completely succumbed to the function of the hangman's noose. James had already lost his bladder up on the scaffold so that wasn't new. His head hung down towards his chest, his mouth was parted, his sloppy tongue was slightly sticking out, his eyes were half closed, and his hands were clenched together behind his back.

I cut James down from the hangman's noose because my stomach was growling in hunger, but I left his body in a contorted pile beneath the gallows. I usually build up a hearty appetite after I murder some poor fool. I went back to 219 after my dinner ritual in the coziness of the tearoom parlor to review the scene I had created and revel in my work. I was too relaxed and weak to drag James heavy corpse to the chute, so I retrieved a trolly and rolled James down to the elevator to take him to down to the basement. To get rid of James's cadaver, I put him in my acid vat for the night. That was a carefully executed, strenuous task with a 190-pound cadaver.

The next day I pulled James's cadaver's skeletal remains out of the acid vat with large steel tongs and placed it on the autopsy table to dry out in front of a fan. The following day James's skeletal remains were dry, so I chopped it up in pieces to fit in a small carton, added disinfectant, and wrapped the carton in plastic. I put the container in the cooler. Next time I go to the county dump, I'll take it with me.

Devil's Dungeon - Postmortem

I call the basement the Devil's Dungeon, sometimes Zone 666. Most of the Blue Pine's guests end up in the Basement where I dispose of their bodies. Underground in the basement I have everything necessary to dispose of a dead body by different methods. It's the most top secret and clandestine floor at the Blue Pine.

If I become sexually or emotionally attached to a visitor, I may keep the cadaver for a time in the cooler. A body part, such as a head or an eye, I will eventually preserve it in plastination or formaldehyde and other chemicals. If I do, that will signify it was an exceptional, unforgettable experience meaning that person was extra special in some way. Occasionally, for a hobby, I experiment on the cadavers organs for something different to do or to keep me busy and out of trouble. I confess, do spend quality time with special cadavers. It all depends on my mood, and the circumstances of why a certain corpse means more to me that others. Every corpse is unique for one reason or another. Each one speaks to me in a different way. There will only be a select few keepsakes I will cherish forever.

The Blue Pine was the first place in my criminal life where I was able to utilize an embalming table for slowly stripping skin off my victim with knives. It is an extremely cruel and painful torture exclusively for a guest I despise. Most guests' remains are disposed of here underground in the acid vat or the oven.

I must write in my journal about an insane experience that I have already had in my Devil's Dungeon.

I recall a woman, Isabel, I took to Room 215. I had planned to cremate her the next day after I murdered her, but when I saw her body at the bottom of the chute, laying there in a heap of bloody flesh, I changed my mind temporarily. I didn't write about this event when I took Isabel into Room 215, the Betty Page Dive, because I didn't have time then, but I'm going to write about it now.

Before I cremated Isabel, I put her body on the embalming table and hosed her off. I cannot admit to feeling any empathy for the woman, but I did feel a connection, so much that I decided to embalm her and make her look as she did when she arrived at the Blue Pine. At this point, I questioned my sanity, my sexuality, and my desires because it didn't make any sense to me, especially because Isabel didn't attract me in the slightest. The more I racked my brain about it, the less sense it made but I carried on in spite of it all.

I had washed Isabel thoroughly with disinfectant, plugged all her orifices, and prepared for an arterial and cavity embalming, then dressed her in the clothes she wore coming here after I washed them to get rid of her blood and feces. Afterwards, I placed her in a cooler compartment temporarily until I decided what pose I would put her in. I still didn't have a reason for why I chose to experiment on Isabel, but it would be a challenge since I had never attempted an extreme embalming alone before. My curiosity is perpetual; with that obsession, I'm frequently exploring unnatural and bizarre deeds that most people wouldn't dare to do. My wild, wicked and innovative schemes and projects keep my deviant mind occupied and distracted. The former owner had left behind enough formaldehyde and other chemicals needed for several more embalming services.

I took Isabel out of the cooler a few hours later and rigor mortis had set in, so I messaged her limbs and joints to make her corpse more easily moveable. I removed her facial peach fuzz, glued her eye lids closed and wired her jaw shut. I sealed her vagina and anus with cotton to prevent fluid leakage as much as possible. But I wanted to do more.

I gave Isabel what my dad called an extreme embalming process. For some reason I was determined to use those same advanced techniques I learned while experimenting on corpses with my dad back in upstate New York.

I had a desire to try my hand at extreme embalming on Isabel and bring her back to her original physical appearance as best as possible because this technique slows down the process of decomposition, therefore preserving the body for a much longer period of time. The first time Dad and I used that process was for the purpose to pose a female corpse of a wealthy lady from the Hamptons. I associated this request with Victorian funerals I had read about. I was satisfied I did a decent job, and it was good practice.

My last experience with dad happened when I was home the summer before going to start at NYU. A Mrs. Stone lost her eighteen-year-old debutant daughter in a fatal boat accident just two days after her high school graduation. Mrs. Stone told dad's boss, the owner of the funeral home, she couldn't bear to see her beautiful daughter lying in a casket. She requested that her daughter Gina be posed in her graduation gown and hat, holding her diploma, standing next to her desk which would have her class textbooks, eyeglasses, and school banner on display. Luckily, the accident didn't ruin Gina's face, so our mortuary makeup artist and cosmetologist who do that part of the restoration art process were able to make her look alive, beautiful and with a slight smile. Dad did a great service with his extreme embalming technique.

Gina was posed standing proudly by her desk like her mother requested. Gina's favorite music that year (1939) was Ella Fitzgerald, so her mum had it playing in the background. We took some photos before the family showed up for the viewing. Numerous graduates from Gina's school came in. Some of them were deeply disturbed by seeing Gina standing and with eyes open, so they didn't walk up close but sat in the back of the reception room crying. Several bold and curious friends approached the scene where Gina was and stared with wild eyes and dropped jaws before bursting out in tears. Only two of Gina's closest friends came up to touch Gina and talk to her. It was a sad scene that those who attended will never forget.

I was asked to stand near Gina's corpse to make sure no one disturbed her. I'm glad I was standing there because Gina's boyfriend Randy came to the viewing extremely intoxicated and wanted to dance with her. It took three of us men to get rid of Randy.

CHAPTER 21

ELLA & FOUR ROSES

It is 1955, almost two years have passed since my last experience was logged in this journal. I got so deeply involved in the daily chores and responsibilities of my Guest Inn business and was overwhelmed by the good luck I started having with my extra-personal activities. Truthfully, I lost interest in keeping this damned journal. Sometimes I'm too tired to write, then too lazy to write, then I make every excuse in the world not to put pen to paper. Ultimately, writer's block set in. I wouldn't have known how to describe what happened to me if an American psychoanalyst hadn't coined and popularized the phrase only five years ago, back in 1947.

Now that I look back, I'm troubled by what happened to me merely because I probably missed putting down in this journal a few novel experiences that should have been documented, however, I'm certain there are plenty of unspeakable events I've already submitted. I'm not alone in my misery about it; writer's block has been a problem throughout recorded history. I avoided writing until I met someone of significance, so I'm writing in this tainted journal again.

A lot has happened since 1953; the year I bought the Blue Pine funeral home and turned it into much more than a mere hotel for guests.

The first two years went well for my new business. I was quite content and secure with my life overall for the first time, but I was missing courting a lady which made no sense to me. I had as many different experiences as I desired and enough for one man to handle, or should I say, enough for one murderer to handle but that hadn't filled the whole void. I had taken exactly two long breaks each year between my favored events because my souvenirs remained powerful longer than usual. When I started taking body parts instead of jewelry and items of clothing, I noticed the fantasy I attached to each one was stronger and lingered for many months longer, so it wasn't mandatory for me to murder a guest as often and I was okay with that. In fact, I welcomed those long standing, powerful fantasies thinking I was mitigating my chances of getting caught.

One beautiful, late afternoon on a Saturday in early June this year, a bonnie lass rang the front doorbell. When I opened the door in my traditional attire, I was taken back by the image that stood before me. She was young, with shiny, platinum blonde hair that glistened in the sunlight, in a short, Italian cut hairstyle, beautiful and perfect. She had the fairest complexion, like the winter's virgin snow with rosy, pink cheeks and crystal blue eyes that twinkled when she smiled. Petite, trim, feminine and soft spoken, she was the whole package. I remember every little detail with my photographic memory because I was spellbound and speechless. I must have stood there in my doorway looking like a fool with wide open eyes and dropped chin. She actually took my breath away. I hadn't seen a vision like that since I was a boy of seventeen back at the funeral home in upstate New York. When I gathered my senses, took a deep breath and shut my mouth, I stepped back, said welcome and the lady into the parlor, up to my desk. I also remember our first conversation together verbatim. It's been stuck in my mind since that glorious day.

"Welcome to my humble abode, young lady." I said, not knowing what to say right away. She was beautiful.

"Please, come in and have a seat here on the settee. Would you join me for a spot of tea?"

I was intent on saying and doing everything in my power to make this beauty feel comfortable.

"Why, yes sir, I'd be delighted to join you. I've had a long day traveling and I would like to relax."

"What is your name, ma'am? Mine is Andrew, Andrew Webb."

"I'm Daisy, Mr. Webb. Daisy Ella Duffie, but I prefer to be called Ella. Daisy sounds so, well, I mean, it sounds rather childish to me."

"That's fine, Ella. Then Ella it is. Duffie is Scottish, isn't it, Ella?"

"Yes, sir. My father is Scottish, and my mum is from Wales. They live in Wales. I'm just here for the summer, the season here, then going home in November. I was told Briggstown was a pleasant little town to stay for the weekend before my journey down to Northeast Harbor where I'll be starting a job next Monday as a waitress at the Asticou Inn."

"The Asticou Inn, you say. That's a fine place. A charming restaurant with a beautiful view of the harbor and Acadia is across the pond. I think you will do well there. I heard a lot of wealthy and famous people stay there."

"Ohhh, that's great news, Mr. Webb. I've never been there."

"Please, call me Andrew. Yes, Andrew."

I wanted this chick to relax and not be formal with me. I made it a point to calm down and relax so I could hit on her in a timely, gentlemanly fashion. I had no time to waste giving my interview. I had to find out more of her personal information before I could make a move. I was eager to flirt and court Ella. I will disclose what I did.

My first move was to excuse myself to go upstairs to quickly change into my best velvet, Victorian power coat, accessories, splash British Sterling on my face and grab my pipe. When I arrived back down to the parlor, Ella was walking around interestedly, looking at my décor.

"I love your Victorian taste, Andrew. It's truly lovely here."

"Yes, Ella, I took great pride in creating this atmosphere for a pretty lady like you to enjoy. Would you care for a tad of brandy in that snifter you're admiring? I have an exquisite tasting bourbon that has a flavor of braised peaches, brown sugar and rye spice I think you will like. It's my 100 proof Four Roses Single Barrel. Try it, you'll like it."

"Ah, and you, Andrew! How dashing you look in that fine garb! I've never seen a man dress like that before."

"Thank you, mi lady. Now, how about joining me for a delicious nightcap."

"Yes, yes, I'd love to, Andrew. It sounds marvelous. It's such a divine occasion to meet a gentleman these days. If you don't mind my asking, where are you from Andrew?"

"Not at all, Ella. Both of my parents came here from England, but I was born in upstate New York." I took a sip of my bourbon and lit my pipe.

"They must have been fine parents to raise such a gentleman as you."

"They were good parents, strict, very strict. How do you like the Four Roses?"

"It's very strong, Andrew, wow. Tasty and spicy like you said, but whoa, it's a heavy hitter. I'm going to have to go slow and easy with this one."

"Take your time pretty lady, twilight is upon us, and the night is young."

I remember distinctly what Ella was wearing. She wore a royal blue, cotton blouse worn tightly against her ample breasts with just a peek of sensuous cleavage peering out over the top of the neckline, a pair of high waisted, navy capri pants and open-toed sandals. Her nails were short, just past her fingertips and painted pink to match her lush lips. As casual as she was, she was beautiful. I wanted her. I lust after her. Patience had to be my virtue, but I would have her. I felt with this lovely young teen, it would be to my advantage to court her as I had done with only one other lady. I haven't had much experience with courtship, but mum had taught me the basics in hopes I would find a nice young lady, fall in love, and get married someday. I'm sure mum died with a broken heart because that never happened. I'm not the marrying kind. I must have my freedom without interference, restrictions or jealousy.

CHAPTER 22

INNKEEPER'S CRUEL COURTSHIP

The moment Ella entered my parlor, I began flirting with her, giving her many compliments and treating her with my personal style of etiquette, like a the noble gentleman I was. Not knowing what kind of music Ella liked, I had gambled and put on my only Tommy Dorsey LP because his band was known for its romantic ballads and smooth sound. It was intended to put Ella in a sentimental, romantic mood if she was so inclined.

"Oh, Andrew, I love the big band sound! It's so romantic."

"I was hoping you liked my choice of music, Ella."

While sipping on the Four Roses, Ella started loosening up and swaying back and forth to the music. That was time to make my next move.

"Would you care to dance, mi lady? May I have your hand in this dance?" I spoke softly and slowly with an encouraging tone to my British accent.

"Yes, I don't mind if we do." Ella seemed relax and trusting.

I took Ella into my arms properly for a slow waltz, not too close at first. I wanted to be able to look deep into her eyes. This is extremely important to start to get to know someone. I was pleased when she caught my gaze and stared deeply back into my eyes. We danced slowly through one side of the album, not talking, just enjoying each other's warm embrace. When the music ended, I turned the record over, turned down the volume for a light background sound for conversation.

"Ella, dear, why don't you have a seat here next to me, and we will lift our snifters once again." I took Ella by the hand and escorted her back to the settee.

"After I finish this flavorsome bourbon, I must call it a night Andrew."

"But we haven't had a chance to talk yet, Ella. Let me add just a drop more to our drinks so we can converse for a little longer."

"I suppose that will be ok, Andrew, but I am getting very tired."

I poured a spot of my best bourbon into both of our snifters and took a seat next to Ella. With other guests, I have a drink or two while interviewing them, but an intended courtship with Ella would be much different. My conversation with her I considered 'grooming talk'. It's a way of exchanging trivial talk of a more intimate nature. I wanted to know Ella's education and background relating to her family and close friend contacts which is like questions I've asked others in an interview.

I felt a distinct, deeper attraction to Ella. I figured the instant attraction to this pretty young lady had to do with my first sexual experience at the age of twelve with Jackie, a seventeen-year-old, blonde beauty who was brought into the funeral Home in New York, dead on the slab. I was exceptionally impressionable at that age, and something sparked in me, and stayed firmly as my type of woman, my type of a deceased woman. Meeting Ella somehow instantly brought a flashback of Jackie to mind. Seeing Ella triggered a memory from the past with a sudden anxiety attack that I had to mask.

I talked with Ella until we finished our drinks. I learned enough about her to feel safe being her suitor or executioner. She was eighteen, graduated from high school and all her family and friends were in Wales. The only information they all had was that her destination was in Northeast Harbor, Maine.

I should have passed up the next phase of my courtship that night, but I didn't. I had already touched her while dancing with her.

I had squeezed her hand and given her a light kiss on the side of her neck at the end of the dance. Nothing more. The first night, I didn't want to push it. I wanted the game of pursuit, the courtship to last longer, so we ended the evening with a brief hug, good nights and I walked Ella up to a guest room on the 3rd floor, two doors down from my private quarters. I wanted this fantasy to last as long as possible, knowing the dance of courtship is different for everybody.

In the morning Ella came down to the tearoom parlor for a Continental breakfast. I greeted her then hugged her firmly but carefully, but this time it was a lingering hug until she gently pushed me away. I didn't clearly understand why I was going through all the courtship steps to make Ella love me because I didn't and would never love her. My narcissistic ego was calling the shots. I concluded I had become lonely and felt unappreciated. I needed the acceptance of another human being; a living human being and I wanted to know if I had lost the attraction women had for me and if I had lost my touch of persuasiveness.

Unknowingly, I was searching for answers. Ella, knowing Ella, seemed to put everything back in perspective for me. Once I realized I was trying to hook Ella to break her heart, I knew what I had been doing subconsciously was in the name of sexual sadism. I wanted her to fall for me so I could laugh at her and tell her she was crazy to fall for a killer. I would thoroughly enjoy her emotional pain and turmoil, so I knew I hadn't deceived myself. For my amusement, I was going about it another way.

I came down to the parlor in a dashing gentleman's morning suit instead of my Victorian attire or casual wear. This debonaire suit has grey and black striped slacks, a grey double-breasted waistcoat, black morning coat, white shirt, and grey ascot. I was dressing to impress my new guest, playing the courtship game, and deflecting monotony.

Dear, sweet Jackie, oh, I mean Ella and I had a cozy get-together over coffee and a raspberry Danish pastry, before she left the Inn to take a tour of Briggstown. I took the day to make plans to continue the masquerade madness I started the night before. Tonight, would be another evening to commit to memory for a long time.

Ella arrived back at the Blue Pine around 6:00 P.M. and I was delighted to greet her in the parlor dressed in my Victorian best. This evening, I was going to flirt more directly because this night was my only option to win the heart of such a pretty las. If I was to fail at making out with her, I would have to change course.

"Good evening, mi lady. How was your day?"

"Fine, thank you, Mr. Webb. I had fun shopping in antique shops along the highway and a I found a white elephant just outside Briggstown."

"That's smashing, Ella. Now, why don't you go to your room and freshen up. I'd like you to join me for a light supper and cocktails this evening."

"That sounds enjoyable, Mr. Webb. I'll change into something more suitable and join you in the parlor in about half an hour."

"Splendid, Jackie, excuse me please, Ella. There I go again. I'm so sorry. I knew a lady once that you remind me of. A delightful lady she was, just like you. Go on, now. I must prepare something for our taste buds. Do you like French Brie and Baguettes, and do you favor champagne? Have you had the pleasure of sipping on Dom Perignon?"

"Oh my, sir, you are so generous and amazing. I've only had the pleasure of tasting delicious French foods and champagne once, at a formal wedding, but I can assure you it wasn't nearly as fine as Dom Perignon! Unfortunately, everything I like is either immoral, indecent, illegal or fattening. Oh, gosh, I shouldn't have said that!"

"Brilliant, Ella, absobloodylootely. Don't get your knickers in a twist. We're just getting to know each other. The evening's supper will be ready soon."

I went to the kitchen and chilled the champagne with joy in my heart. I believe she made a Freudian slip which was encouraging to me. I knew it wasn't a lot of bunk. Though I had never engaged in a traditional courtship before, this was my modus operandi for courtship. I was having a whale of a time with this newly acquired interest. I had no idea what Ella thought of my presentations, but I was certain she was having fun, too. I knew this young las had never experienced anything like Andrew and his performance. An hour flew by before Ella joined me in the parlor, but I was patiently waiting and prepared.

"I'm so sorry I'm later than you expected, Mr. Webb. I wanted to bathe and put on something nice tonight for such an exceptional invitation for supper."

"How lovely you look this evening, mi lady. Please have a seat here and I'll pour you a chilled glass of Dom Perignon. There. Enjoy it. Let's have a toast." Saying that, Ella lifted her glass to tap mine before taking a sip, as I expected.

"Mmmm, that's superb, Mr. Webb. What a wonderful treat. Thank you."

I excused myself and went to the small icebox behind the bar in the parlor to retrieve the small platter of French Brie and slices of Baguette. I was hoping this informal rendezvous wouldn't turn into a crum-a-grackle. I conscientiously poured on my British accent to give this pretty, young las 'the whole hog' of an experience which might be her last. I wasn't sure that evening how long I was going to carry on with my charade. I had turned on music in the background before Ella entered the parlor to play one of my French albums, 'La Vie Parisienne.' I had prepared a cozy ambiance fit for a Queen. It was 'ace'. I was doing well with this courtship thing, but my goal was another story. Towards the end of this night's supper, after a couple glasses of Champagne and a few shots of Four Roses 100 proof, I was getting sauced and I hoped it was getting closer to the time to bring Ella's courtship to another level.

CHAPTER 23

A BLESSING VS. A CURSE

The early evening hours had passed quickly with hours of conversation about English and French literature, the classics in music and art and a debate about formal education both private and public. I was extremely impressed with the amount of knowledge this young lass had already obtained at a young age. It was a thrilling experience for me to have an in-depth, intellectual conversation after too long without any, my brain had been starved for this sort of stimulation. I hadn't had the opportunity to delve deeply into these particular subjects with other intellectuals since my university days.

It concerned me for a time that I had started to stress about what Ella's limitless value and contribution to society would be as she aged. I saw this as both a blessing and a curse to know her because she possessed such an extraordinary mind and ultimate capacity to achieve anything she aspired to. For the first time in my life, my feelings about a human being were in conflict. I was shocked I had the capability to have a conflict of interest about Ella. I had no love or affection for her. I had no present sexual attraction to her. I liked her gifted mind, that's all. I admired and appreciated her brilliance and educational aptitude. I told myself that's all it was, until I flipped to face the reality, I had the intention, need, and power to extinguish her; to snuff her out like the flame of the candle on the mantel. For selfish reasons, I would be destroying something great that was only in its early development. My unfamiliar dilemma should not be problematic to me. This conflict, in and of itself, was unlike me. This was ridiculous. Was it the liquor that had confused my mind? I normally don't get intoxicated. I wasn't sure about anything that night, so I thought it was in my best interest to put my immoral desires on hold and call it a night. Tomorrow, tomorrow, blessed it would be tomorrow if this all appears to have been a bad dream. A Saturday night's nightmare or will it have been a mysterious and fearful dream.

CHAPTER 24

BETRAYAL & BLISS

Sunday morning passed without me. I woke up with a pulsing headache in the early afternoon. I vaguely remembered being in a miserable quandary the night before. It was a faint blur. Nothing bothered me today, so I blamed the bad dream on having plenty of welly. I bathed and dressed in a short time so I could check up on Ella. I remembered she had planned to check out today, so I had to catch her before she vacated the Blue Pine premises. I took my elevator down to the first floor and hurried to the parlor just in time to see Ella leaving a note at the front desk.

"Good afternoon, Ella. You weren't leaving before saying goodbye, were you? I apologize; I slept in too late today. I admit, I had a tad too much of the good spirits last night. How do you feel, mi lady?"

"I feel fine today, Mr. Webb and thank you for a fantastic Saturday night. I'm checking out, but I promise to come back to visit now and then. It was a pleasure to have such a great conversation. I learned a lot from you."

"My pleasure, indeed, Ella, my pleasure entirely. But you must stay just for a few more minutes to have a tad of café and a croissant with me before you travel. You shouldn't be leaving on an empty stomach; besides, this is how we can say goodbye. Please stay just for a little brunch. I do have fresh orange juice as well, so I could make a couple of refreshing Mimosas with the left-over champagne to give us a bit of 'the hair of the dog', if you know what I mean?"

"Oh, well, okay, Mr. Webb, you are very convincing. But I can only stay for an hour, no more, because I want to get to Mount Desert before dark."

"Blooming brilliant, mi lady. Go have a seat in the tearoom. I will retrieve the juice and croissants from the kitchen's icebox and make our Mimosas. I will return momentarily. Make yourself at home."

I had a bitter hangover for the first time since my university days, but I recall every conversation I had with Ella. I went to the kitchen to make the Mimosas in privacy. Just before I completed my mission, Ella appeared at the kitchen's doorway asking if she could help in any way. I told her,

"Yes, yes indeed, my dear lady. Take this tray into the parlor and check by the front door for Sunday's Bangor Daily News. I like to sit on the porch on nice days and leisurely read the newspaper. That's how I spend Sunday afternoons."

"Of course, Mr. Webb. I'd be happy to."

Off she went, so I could do my dirty deed. I quickly took my stash of arsenic and deposited a fatal dose of 180 mg. into one of the Mimosas. I knew the brainchild wouldn't be able to smell or taste it and the dose she would ingest would be fatal in a few hours. In the meantime, until she passed, she would suffer in pain, nausea, vomiting and bloody diarrhea. That's the gross part. I prepared myself for Ella's disgusting ending.

"Here you are, my dear. Let's make a toast to our forever friendship. To us, bottoms up!"

Ella tapped my glass of Mimosa, nodded her head in agreement and took a large swallow of the yellow concoction, a bite of the croissant, then another swig of the delightful death drink. She smiled and winked at me in thanks.

"Tastes good this way, Mr. Webb. I like the croissant, too."

I had served the fair, blonde teenager a small gold plate with a warm croissant, butter and strawberry preserves beside it. To make sure my strategy succeeded, I had mixed some arsenic in the preserves as well. This deadly brunch couldn't fail. No more failures for me at the Blue Pine. I'm still haunted by what happened with Jerry in 203.

While we were slowly and delicately eating and not saying much, someone came to the front door. I excused myself thinking 'of all times' this wasn't a good time. The bloke at the door was a waiter passing through. I told him there was no vacancy; he should try at the motel down the road. I went back to the parlor in haste to see how the brilliant lass was doing. She was just finishing her drink, so I offered her the café.

"Yes, I believe I will, thank you, sir. This drink went down too fast, so I'll have some café to finish the rest of my croissant. By the way, this jam is delicious. You sure have a knack for entertaining with food and beverages, Mr. Webb."

"Thank you kindly, my dear. I do my best. Would you care for another pastry? I have one more left with your name on it."

"No, thank you, Mr. Webb. One of these is quite enough. Just perfect."

I sat patiently for about thirty minutes talking to Ella and watching her actions closely before she started complaining of abdominal pain and nausea. I asked her if she wanted some Pepto-Bismol for her symptoms and she couldn't say thank you enough. I gave her plenty of it, knowing it wouldn't help at all.

Another twenty minutes flew by, and Ella was feeling much worse. She complained of severe muscle cramps, and tingling in her fingers and toes.

Oddly, this brought to mind my grandmother telling mum and showing her an old ad in the Sears Roebuck & Co., Inc. Catalog. that read: 'Dr. Rose's Complexion Wafers' Chicago, Ill.,1902. This product was sold to clear up skin on a woman's face. They said, imagine that? Sears & Roebuck are selling bizarre and dangerous products! I remembered seeing the ad because my brain took a photograph of it. Enough of that unnecessary side note.

The afternoon became the early evening while my unfortunate guest was spending most of the time in the loo, vomiting and with diarrhea. I expected this night would be unpleasant, but it was worse than unpleasant. It was disgusting and I was miserable.

The first floor reeked of putrid smells. Eventually, I coaxed Ella to go back to her room while she could still walk. I put an empty coffee can by her bedside and locked her bedroom door. I left her alone to pass away during the night from dehydration and shock. Writing this will undoubtedly show everyone what a vicious, sadistic murderer I am. I'm guilty and I know I'm a deadly monster.

Later that night, I went over to Ella's room to check on her condition. When I went in, I was surprised to find her still alive but barely breathing. She was having seizures and saliva was drooling out of the corners of her mouth, rushing down her cheeks. Her clothes were soaked with sweat and soiled. I tried to talk to her, but she was delirious and grunting sounds I didn't understand. She wasn't capable anymore to talk or rationalizing. I was about to walk out of the room, my precocious young guest started having convulsions, so I thought she was near death, but not sure. I wanted this new day to play out better and faster than this, so I turned around with a change of heart. I altered my scheme. I pulled the pillow out from under her golden locks, put it over her face and smothered her to death. In about ninety seconds, she stopped thrashing around and stopped breathing. I lifted the pillow to find a horrible facial expression. Ella's eyes were wide open, her mouth was open, and she was staring straight at me with the most frightful face I had ever seen. Done. The sight of her horrifying expression will stay in my mind's eye until the day I die. I believe that's my karma.

It was time to get on with my busy night cleaning up and taking ugly Ella to the Devil's Dungeon, the morgue, my basement. I stopped short in my tracks. Wait, I couldn't do any of that yet. What was I thinking? I must have gotten temporarily distracted from this afternoon's parlor scene. My sweet, young, blonde girl, my dear Jackie was right here waiting for me, nice and warm. Umm. I hadn't had any café or a slice of black pudding yet, but after I shag Jackie, I'll be ready for a full English breakfast. Yes, three fried eggs, sausages, tomatoes, mushrooms, and fried bread. I'm hungry, so let's get this over with.

"Come to daddy my pretty Jackie. It's overdue that we have some quality time together. I've been patiently waiting since I first met you when you walked through the front door of the Blue Pine."

I spoke to, oh, I've been calling Ella, Jackie. She reminded me so much of the first time I shagged a booty at seventeen. A warm corpse's booty at the funeral home I grew up in. It really doesn't matter who I call what. Jackie, Ella, they're all dead. All that matters is that I get what I want and need. Last night ended with my betrayal of Ella. Tonight, it will end with my sexual bliss.

CHAPTER 25

VICTORIAN FUNERAL

After my sexual appetite was sufficed, I lounged in the comfortable chair in my cozy parlor sipping on a cup of café and indulging in an abundant dish of Black Pudding while puffing deeply on my pipe. I was relaxed, teary-eyed and celebrating my achievement. My time with Ella was more superb compared to anything I had engaged in for a long time. I couldn't remember the last time I felt so relieved, sentimental and euphoric all at the same time. But I also reminisced about my first time being intimate with a female, Jackie, that was inexplicably heavenly. I depended on that experience to get me off for years. Not that I hadn't been active with others during that time frame, but Jackie topped them all. I've never forgotten my first.

I dozed off with a full belly for a couple of hours and woke up energized and keen to taking Ella to the basement. No one else was staying at the Blue Pine so I wrapped her body up in a blanket and carried her to the elevator. Once in the morgue, I laid her stinking corpse on the embalming table and prepared the special potion of chemicals for embalming I had learned from my father. I was compelled to preserve the female that reminded me of my first love. I may never have this opportunity again. I am going to be able to keep courting Jackie soon in the style and creation that pleases me for as long as it takes to fulfill those wishes. Until then, I will be taking care of business down here and upstairs for the Blue Pine Guest Inn. I may permit a male to spend a day or two for some extra revenue because I'm not certain what the total of expenditures for my new project will accrue.

I found the perfect casket, still in a box among the others that were left behind. I tore open one end of the box so I could see the casket. The outside was a shimmering gold and the lining on the inside was a soft, yellow velveteen. There were yellow roses embroidered on the inside of the front half's top. There was an invoice taped on the box that read, 'Golden Casket, Ordered for Giorgio Marcello and in parenthesis (Mary). Dated Arrived December 20, 1952. Balance due. This superior piece was a special order for a wealthy family, because the price said over $25,000. When I read that, I hurried to cut the rest of the box open to get a good look at this handsome piece. It was sitting majestically under a faint spotlight, so it glowed like a gold bullion. I had never seen a casket so beautiful in every way. I wondered what had happened. Why hadn't this gorgeous casket been used for Mary? I assume Mr. Marcello went all out because Mary must have been either Giorgio's wife or precious daughter and the funeral was set December 24th. I'll ask my realtor if he knew the story, but I'm going to guess the funeral home wasn't able to perform funeral services for this family because the Blue Pine's funeral director was sick or had passed away. Their loss and my gain because nothing is too expensive for the love of my life.

My initial chore was to scrub Jackie's filthy body from face to feet and massage every inch of her body to soften the rigor to give her the dignity she deserved. After I thoroughly cleaned her, I set her mouth, by wiring her jaw shut and replaced her eyes with crystal blue, artificial eyes. I punctured her organs and removed all fluids and gas and filled her hollow organs and empty spaces with embalming fluid. I fixed a slight smile, no teeth showing, and open eyes which is what I prefer. Then she was ready for the final process embalming process, my father's unique embalming system.

Embalming by arterial injection as a mortuary practice thought to have begun in my home country in the 1700s. However, I performed a superior embalming process on my pretty girl to prevent her from decomposing for an extended period. I did it exactly the way dad taught me. While her blood was draining and being replaced with a formaldehyde mixture (to keep her skin from turning brown and shriveling all over), I went upstairs to prepare myself a cocktail, platter of bloody, rare roast beef and creamy mashed potatoes. When I finished eating and drinking enough red wine and smoking my pipe for a while out on the porch, I figured Jackie would have gotten back to looking lifelike.

I also learned the art of cosmetics and enhancement under my dad, so I intended to bring Jackie back to her lovely complexion, to her lifelike state. I brushed her long, gorgeous blonde hair taking long, slow strokes and bending down to smell her essence while I stared into her liquid blue eyes. What I plan to do with her corpse will likely disturb most people who may read this journal. But that's not my concern.

My father learned on his own by experiments on corpses by trial and error on how to embalm a body to last longer than traditional embalming. That wealthy lady's request I mentioned earlier was responsible for dad taking on the challenge. We did and it worked. She paid us well. That being stated, today was an important day for me to be able to apply this method to Jackie. It may be the first and last time and I will make a perfect, lifelike, life size doll of Jackie so I can continue to court her and have my love wherever and whenever I choose the way I choose. I wish Jackie could live with me forever, at least as long as possible.

CHAPTER 26

ENGLISH TEA PARTY

It's time to check on Jackie. Her blood should have drained out of her body, so I can continue with her extraordinary preparation. Jackie will get the royal treatment of embalming. You'll see. My creative juices are flowing now, and this will be as much of a challenge as a fun job for me.

"Oh, Jackie, dear, here I come, sweetheart. Andrew is on his way to take care of you."

Yes, I talk to Jackie and I'm sure she appreciates me. Voices in my head talk to me frequently and I talk to Jackie every time I'm with her. We discussed her sleeping arrangements and I told her I don't feel a casket is an appropriate resting place for her, only at certain times when I'm busy upstairs. But I have better plans for my love which are not for the faint of heart. I don't see Jackie as a lifeless corpse like others would and she won't look like a corpse when I finish with her. I'm not a mortuary makeup artist but I learned from watching it being done numerous times at the funeral home I grew up in. I know I've already said that. I've learned most of my craft by watching, some by reading and a lot by doing. My curiosity got the best of me, so I took advantage of learning the skill and tonight I plan to put it to good use. I won't go into much more details about cleaning her body, cleaning up all released body fluids, plugging her orifices, wiring her jaw or plumping closed excluding her eyes. I will take my time to complete everything the way I want it. Then I will come back and write more. If I sound wacky to you, I'm guilty as charged.

I'm back and ready to apply cosmetics to Jackie's face. Her skin is back to her natural tone now and soon her face will have rosy cheeks and lips, and a little eye makeup. I have Jackie propped up, sitting up in a high back chair. I put a thin metal rod through her back, neck and into the base of her skull to secure her. I can sit with her while applying makeup. I brought a small case of that special makeup from dad's supplies after he died.

I dressed Jackie in a chic, full-length white wedding dress, formerly my mother's. It was far too big for her, so I folded it behind her and stitched it up with a large postmortem autopsy needle with the same heavy thread as I have used to suture a large incision after a forensic examination. It worked and looks creepy but no one but my eyes will see it. I put a gold sash over Jackie's shoulders and loosely around her neck. She is ready to join me for tea in my parlor. But first, I must prepare the necessities for the formal Victorian tea party. I've been looking forward to seeing it before I escort my love to the parlor. She will wait patiently until I'm ready.

"Here we are my dear. Have a seat right here next to me on this sweet velvet settee. I will put on the music I find romantic and pour a spot of tea for each of us, darling."

I sat down next to Jackie, took her cold stiff hand and held it gently in my warm palm while I sipped my tea. I talked to her for hours and it seemed that I couldn't hold my eyes open any longer. We shared a lovely evening together in a comfortable romantic atmosphere. I held her close and kissed her cheek and neck before taking her to my room for the night. Tonight, she will sleep with me because this night resembled our wedding night. It wasn't desirable, nor necessary for me to engage in sexual activity with Jackie on this cherished, celebratory evening, but I felt it was my responsibility to make her feel secure and loved. Tomorrow is another day.

I was awake bright and early and it was strange to feel a cold stiff lying next to me, then I gathered my senses and remembered it was Jackie. I lay there with voices and thoughts running through my mind. They kept saying to me, "Fuck the bloody whore in your bed, you deranged lunatic! She's laying there waiting for you, anxious for you; she needs you! Make her warm, Andy boy, put her flimsy body on heating pads and fuck her!" But I kept shaking my head, hitting my head, trying to ignore those ugly loud voices.

"No, no!" I yelled out loud to the voices in my head. "You're the lunatics, leave me alone!" But they wouldn't shut up, they kept screaming at me, dictating to me to fuck the dead whore, but I'm not going to listen to them this time. I jumped out of bed and ran downstairs to the kitchen to make some café and clear my head. I had to get away from them and divert my attention to anything else, anything. Maybe a guest will come to the door today. That would be nice. I need to talk to someone in the living flesh, so I won't lose my mind. I was shaking, sweating, and breathing heavy out of nerves, anxiety and anger. Damn, I'm okay, I know I'm okay, but those terrible, ugly voices ordering me to do terrible things have to be silenced. I cannot let them interfere with my plans. They must go away and leave me alone!

I sat in the parlor alone, writing in this journal, having my café, forcing down a Danish pastry, thinking, planning, and being concerned if those voices would eventually rule me. My double life has always been complicated, so I don't need this extra turmoil. I sat there toking on my pipe until I had my wits about me. In an hour or so, I cleaned up all the bits and bobs in the parlor from my rendezvous the night before with Jackie and my morning's breakfast mess.

I know by now you, the reader must have diagnosed me. I'm aware I'm a multi-faceted queer bird. You either like me, or you don't. There's no in-between.

As time goes on chances are you may be more shocked than you already are. You see I'm going to do something I've never done before. I'm going to keep Jackie to be my companion for as long as possible. Though I've done a thorough, extra special embalming of Jackie, she will eventually start to decay. When I can't handle her decomposition; when she starts to look repulsive and unappealing, I will go to Plan B. In the evenings, I will put her to bed in her own special cooler drawer downstairs in Zone 666. I lined Jackie's drawer with a pink velvet material and put a small pillow under her head. I must keep her comfortable.

My plan. I want Jackie to accompany me doing different lifestyle things like having dinner with me, watching TV and I going for an occasional ride in the hearse. Maybe we'll have a picnic in

Acadia National Park. I haven't decided whether she will be riding next to me or laying down peacefully in the back. If someone approaches the hearse when she is sitting in the front seat, I will merely tell the person she's has a bit of motion sickness and not feeling very well, so I'm letting her rest undisturbed until we head back home. I know what to do.

That afternoon, I cleaned out the dining room and prepared a formal dining table setting with sterling silverware, two candelabras and linen napkins. On special occasions, I will have Jackie join me for a candlelight evening. I'll never know what it's like to have a living, breathing wife, but this is as close as it will get; she's the perfect alternative for me. No complaints, no backtalk, pure silence.

CHAPTER 27

INNKEEPER'S MOCK MARRIAGE

"You are looking fine looking woman, m 'lady. You look prettier than all the others in your elegant, vintage wedding dress. I'm going to make it official between you and me. I have a big surprise for you, Jackie, so have a seat on this chair. There you are. On my bended knee here, Jackie, will you be my wife?"

I'm not irrational enough to think she could have responded, but I went through the motions for my own pleasure and I'm sure she heard me. I took her delicate hand and kissed it gently. There were no witnesses, no preacher, or guests present. Just Jackie and me. I put my mother's wedding ring carefully on her left-hand ring finger, and it fit perfectly with a little push. I picked up her veil and kissed her lightly on her cold lips and caressed her cheek. I sat her in the wheelchair and took her up to the parlor on the first floor for a celebratory drink and some classical music. I broke out my best champagne, the only bottle of Krug in my collection that I had been saving for a grande celebration. After all, this was a unique occasion.

Jackie was so ravishing I couldn't take my eyes or hands off her. I just wished at that time, that night she had been warm to me for our wedding night. After our quiet celebration alone, I took Jackie upstairs in the elevator to my suite. I carried her over the threshold and laid her down on my bed. I lay awake for a few minutes pondering the evening's event until the flutes of Krug put me to sleep.

CHAPTER 28

HONEYMOON TO DIE FOR

The next morning, Jackie had a Continental breakfast with me, and we discussed honeymoon plans. My dearest wanted to go to see Niagara Falls but my parents had taken me there as a child when we lived in upstate New York, so I won the discussion, and we decided to stay in Maine. I took Jackie for a nice leisurely ride down to the big island so she could feel the cool, ocean breeze against her face riding up to the top of Cadillac Mountain.

We sat in the car with the windows down taking in the breathtaking view for over an hour, parked as far away from other cars as possible. I noticed there were a lot of curiosity seekers looking at the hearse, mumbling and motioning to those they were with. One young couple hand in hand on their honeymoon came up to my window and peered in telling me they thought our ride was super cool. The young bride peered in at Jackie and introduced herself and asked how she was doing. I explained she didn't feel well from being motion sickness from the ride up, so she wasn't talking. The polite couple wished us a great vacation and then went on their way to do their sightseeing. I was convinced they thought Jackie was being still because of illness.

Leaving beautiful Acadia, we took another leisurely drive down to Bar Harbor and stopped for an ice cream sundae at a quaint little place just on the outskirts of town. We sat in the car to enjoy our ice cream, but I was annoyed about how many curious patrons had to come up close to take a look at the hearse. Times like that makes me thankful for dark tinted windows. I drove my lady slowly back to Briggstown as the sunlight was turning to darkness.

At home, we sat in the hearse behind the Blue Pine holding hands for a short time looking at the captivating full silvery moon and making wishes for the future. I took her wheelchair out of the back of the hearse and secured Jackie in the seat. I park behind the building in front of the garage and use the rear entrance where we come and go without drawing the attention of nosey neighbors. I've had good luck so far.

Our short, but cozy honeymoon was enough for me, and Jackie had no complaints. That's one of the things I love about her. She never gives me a hard time and is easy to please, unlike all other women. She's the best.

I put Jackie to bed that night in her comfy coffin. I knew she'd be comfortable there, lying on the plush and tufted velvet. I kissed her forehead, bid her a good night and left the basement. I had something on my mind that I couldn't shake off, so I had to go into the parlor, take a nightcap of 43, smoke my pipe and muse for a while about my latest crazy and creative idea.

CHAPTER 29

ANDREW'S WEB

An interesting chap came into the Blue Pine later that week to request a three-night stayover. I gladly rented my guest suite to this lively fellow and cheerfully entertained him on his arrival. I hadn't had a good soul talk to another bloke for a while, so I was anxious to converse with him over some Jim Beam. Curtis seemed like a nice man, well-mannered and easy to talk to. He was nursing a broken heart from his last love who had dumped him on Valentine's Day that year. I listened and consoled him until he broke out in tears. This is how I bonded with him to make him feel at home in the Blue Pine. You might define what I do as 'grooming.'

"Have another drink, my good man. All this misery will fade in the future. My advice is, never trust a woman. They're all bitches. The living ones are too much trouble, and you will never know if they're being truthful., so I stay away."

"What do you mean 'the living' ones, Andrew?"

"Oh, nothing, Curtis. I was just referring to women, you know, all women. They're all a pain in the bum. I gave them up years ago. You'll see what I mean someday. You're too young to have experienced much of it yet."

"Why don't we call it a night, get some sleep and you'll feel better in the morning, okay Curtis? The night tends to be depressing for people who have lost a loved one. Tomorrow in the bright sunlight your pain won't feel so devastating."

"Yes, Andrew, that sounds like a plan. I feel drowsy and can't keep my eyes open anymore. I think I had too much to drink but thank you for your hospitality."

Curtis was falling into my web of deception without any resistance. He had fervently chugalugged a few Jim Beam with coke that I had spiked from my stash of barbiturates. He slumped back into the chair in the parlor, barely awake. I left him there and went to get the wheelchair. I needed Curtis to help me with my latest creation, so I bypassed taking him to one of my torture rooms and wheeled him straight down to the basement to the Devil's Dungeon. The basement was going to proudly wear its name tonight. I wheeled Curtis into the elevator which had barely room enough for both of us.

I hoisted him up onto the embalming table with my lift, to lay him out there temporarily. I removed his ring and watch. I liked his college ring, so I kept it for a trophy.

I didn't take time preparing his body before I placed it into the cremation container. He was wearing his clothes and still breathing when I rolled his big body over to the flaming hot cremation chamber. He woke up for a minute when the horrid heat burned his skin, but just long enough to let out a horrible scream when the violent flames hugged his face and torso. I smiled to myself, closed the door and came over here to write about it in my journal. He didn't suffer long so my thrills were short-lived, because I had a new project on my mind and I was eager to see how it would work. I left him in the oven for almost three hours because of his size. I spent most of that time talking to Jackie and reading. When the deadly inferno had reduced Curtis to bone fragments and parts of a skull, I swept those remains up into a shovel-like scoop, used a sledgehammer to pound down the big skull pieces, then I emptied all the bone content into the big blender, the bone grinder, the emulsifier. This heavy-duty machine ground down Curtis's remains into tiny bone fragments and ashes. I purposely left a good portion of tiny bone fragments, so I'd have more bulk material for my project.

After the cremation process was completed, I went over to kiss Jackie good night. I didn't want to do this, but I felt it was necessary to slide my dear Jackie into the mortuary fridge for 24 – 48 hours while I worked on my new project. I hurried to my suite to write and reflect.

The next day I took a day trip to Bangor to go shopping for some attractive throw pillows for my new pillow project. I found three small velvet pillows, about 8" x 8" square: two in burgundy and one in a deep rose pink. That was all I needed to get this mission going. I was delighted to find the colors I needed.

The traveling day passed by quickly and night fell upon me before I arrived home. I was weary, tired and looked forward to a peaceful evening with my pipe and a large cup of Espresso. Jackie would have to be patient because my ambition tonight was to work on my project until the café no longer had effects. I sat comfortably in the parlor just as the clock chimed 9:00 PM. Yawning profusely at first, but I was able to cut a sizable opening in one of the burgundy pillows and remove some of the foam. I went down to Zone 666 to retrieve Cutis's ashes and a large funnel, then back upstairs to the kitchen to grab a quick ham & cheese on Rye with yellow mustard and then back to the parlor to continue.

I scoffed down my sandwich and sipped on the Espresso until I got a burst of energy, so I could feel motivated to keep going. I used the big metal funnel to carefully empty the bag of Cutis's ashes into a burgundy pillow. I mixed up the contents in the pillow, then stitched up the opening. Ahh, there it was and brilliant if I must say so for myself. A trophy pillow! I wish I had thought of this years ago. This would be an extraordinary way to keep mementos of a loved one; to keep a loved one close, extremely close. Or a favorite pet. Not for me, but it would work for a pet, too. I know this pillow tribute would be terribly macabre for most people. But think of the bright side. You could hug the pillow, sleep with the pillow, or lay your cheek against it to feel close to someone or something. For me, it's an exclusive and secretive alternative for keeping souveniers.

CHAPTER 30

'PILLOW TALK' IN THE MORGUE

I was enthralled with my trophy pillow idea, in fact, I got my second wind to spend some intimate time with Jackie. I put the burgundy pillow against the back of the settee and rushed down to the basement. I pulled out the drawer where Jackie had been resting and rolled her corpse over to the autopsy table, so I could talk to her.

"How is my sweetheart tonight? Did you have a nice nap? I missed you so much, baby. It's been over 24 hours and that's too long, don't you think, my love. Shhh, no honey, you don't have to answer. I'm sorry I had to put you in that cold, dark place. It must have been frightening for you to be alone in that gloomy drawer, but I'll make it up to you, I promise. How would you like to spend some time with me tonight? You would have been fond of Curtis, Jackie. It's unfortunate you didn't have a chance to meet him, but he'll always be close to us in the parlor, you'll see. I want to have some quality time with you here. You look so beautiful lying there in your wedding dress. I'm going to put a heating pad, maybe two on your body for a very short time, just long enough for us to have some love. I know it won't warm you up, but if I feel the heat against my body it might help. I'm going to try it to see it will assist in my desire for you."

I'm certain this journal isn't going to sit well with most people, but there are many people that favor abnormal and bizarre sexual activities. I know I'm not the only one.

I plugged my extra-large heating pad into the socket near the table and placed it over Jackie's body from her bust to her genitalia. I couldn't keep it on her for long because I didn't want to instigate decomposition. I only wanted to take the chill off her corpse for a few minutes so I could get turned on in a hurry. I pulled myself up onto the autopsy table like I did decades ago at the funeral home in

New York when Jackie was delivered to us from the county morgue. Since then, since that day, I have never gotten over fantasizing about her. She was my first and only love.

The heating pad warmed her dress enough, so I couldn't resist having my way with Jackie. I slowly pulled up her dress, mounted her and injected myself into her private parts which had been lurking under her satin and lace gown. I wasn't happy she felt cold inside, but it had to suffice. I shagged her with a performance of precision like it was Jackie and I called out her name throughout. I honestly felt my sex act was precise enough to give instructions in necrophiliac intercourse and lovemaking. If a man like me never shared his complex sexuality and most intimate needs and experiences, most of the world would be left in a naïve darkness of obliviousness or denial.

Getting back to shagging Jackie, I had a delightful evening with her that night because my little unwanted friends didn't come to interrupt me. I have pretended so intensely with Ella since I met her that I only see Jackie. I'm not sure if I'll shag her corpse after the cooler again, but I could be happy seeing her and touching her while I masturbate on her. I'm counting on the extreme embalming keeping Jackie presentable and doable for as long as possible. Research has stated it can potentially last for several months under ideal conditions. With use of the cooler, I expect a long, erotic and romantic marriage.

CHAPTER 31

BLUE PINE'S 'FOREVER' KEEPSAKES

To be clear, like 'agony and ecstasy,' one person's pain is another person's pleasure. Another year has passed. I decided not to write for a while for the simple reason, I didn't want to be repetitive about my activities on the second floor. Each event was slightly different but not dramatic enough to write about. To sum it up briefly, during the past eleven months, I thoroughly and delightfully entertained several of my most appealing guests in rooms 201 – 219.

My favorite torture rooms now are 201, the H.H. Holmes Gas Chamber; 211 Necktie Party, and Zone 666, the Devil's Dungeon. I have had the most amazing experiences in those rooms; however, I can't complain about the other torture room activities.

During last year's escapades, two of my male guests and two female guests ended up in my private crematorium, so I would have a substantial amount of crushed and pulverized bones and ashes for more trophy pillows. The final resting place for Edgar, Chester, Lula and Viola will each be in the comfort of a plush, silk or velvet pillow with their name embroidered on it. My stuffing pillows project for sales will start this year. Customers, families of their dearly departed will have a choice of burial containers; a casket, an urn, a pine box or a small pillow with the deceased person's name, birth year and death year embroidered on the pillow of their choice.

Now, I'll fill in what has happened in my life over the past year. The first part of last year I courted my bride. We enjoyed two candlelight dinners, a drive through the big park, two cocktail parties in the parlor and a picnic on a lake, but sadly, Jackie's body started decomposition after about three weeks from her death. Regretfully, I couldn't delay the process any longer. I blamed it on the fluids. I believe my custom embalming fluid didn't have enough of the chemicals needed for a lengthy preservation or it was missing one or more critical chemicals. Now that I think about it, dad's custom embalming fluid was expected to last only a few weeks or a month.

When I saw what had started, I spent one last night relishing every minute and adoring Jackie for hours and talking to her, knowing the next day the love of my life would be reduced to a mound of ashes for a pretty pillow. At first, I put Jackie in a beautiful urn that was left behind until I had enough free time to find the perfect pillow. I searched for a few months and found nice pillows for the four guests I had favored and eventually I found the final resting place for my dearest Jackie. I feel more balanced now. I can take Jackie with me wherever I go, and she will be beside me in bed at night. Good night, my love.

CHAPTER 32

INNKEEPER'S NIGHTMARE

My third year at the Blue Pine Guest Inn has brought disturbing concerns I must pay attention to. I figured my life would take a drastic turn someday.

During the Christmas holidays, I sensed something was wrong but had no proof of my suspicions. I started noticing strange things happening. For one, it looked like someone had disturbed the contents of my garbage bin behind the Inn. The next odd thing was that too many people were coming to my door at all different times asking questions about my operation and the overnight accommodations. Their questions were fishing for information. I also started receiving phone calls asking about availability, rates and house rules at the Blue Pine. Not like the first two years, all of a sudden people seemed too curious about what was going on here.

It was New Years Day, January 1, 1956, my third year at the Blue Pine when I decided to ride out this bad storm of my instincts for a few more months. I would be living with high risk by staying, but I needed to identify if it was just my imagination, or to see if everything would go back to normal.

I had delt with Code Enforcement and licensing before I opened and had been paying taxes when they were due, so it wasn't any of that. A few months in seemed too quiet. From super busy with inquiries to silence is a red flag to me, so my suspicions turned to paranoia. My gut feelings told me to get the hell out of Briggstown. Quickly.

I started planning to abandon the Blue Pine, but I knew it would take a decisive strategy to be able to bow out of this community and business gracefully, quietly and unnoticed. If that was possible, it would be a miracle.

It took three months of silence into 1956 before I saw more signs I wasn't safe here anymore. It's the first time in my lifetime, I have felt this much pressure of being discovered, police getting too close and I don't like how I feels. I thought maybe my phone was being wire tapped. I wondered if someone saw something they thought looked mysterious, so they reported it to the town's law enforcement, who in turn started an investigation of the Blue Pine. I hadn't heard anything lately about the manhunt for the Necktie Strangler in New York City and the Boston area, so I was hoping those investigations had become cold cases. I haven't been operating in Briggstown with the same MO I used down south of here years ago, so it wasn't likely these local authorities had made the connection. What startled me was waking up to an alarming announcement in the local newspaper. On the front page in big, bold print it said:

"**Manhunt Underway**, keep you doors locked and don't walk anywhere alone. The chief of police got on a television station out of Bangor and stated he believed there was a killer on the loose in the Briggstown area. We have organized an around-the-clock search for a 'mad slayer', a murderer, and we have reason to believe this fiend is armed and dangerous and has already murdered several people. The Ellsworth police department are working closely and coordinating with us and law enforcement all the way up to Bangor and law enforcement in Augusta have offered help."

Later that same morning, the TV news station at 11:00 A.M. in Bangor broadcasted the same warning I read in the local newspaper and in the Bangor Daily News. I dropped by the Long Drink to see if I'd hear any gossip. It was about 1:00 PM when Mel turned on the news station. The chief of police warned the community again to stay vigilant because there was a dangerous killer near, and they didn't know when or where he would strike again. He also said a couple of teenagers were shooting rats at the dump the night before and discovered a torn bag full of body parts. Mel reached up and changed the station on the bar's TV. He told the few of us sitting at the bar that his buddy in this police district told him today that the discovery instigated an immediate detailed search through garbage bags at the dump. He also said, sadly this morning they found the badly decomposed remains of four dismembered human bodies in separate bags and one bag with two mutilated rats. They were going to route through as many bags as possible until dark and tomorrow, deliver the bags to the forensic lab at the State of Maine Prison in Thomaston, Maine. I wasn't surprised about that, because I had heard recently that the lab there was considered one of the best and largest in the state. They were I must play it cool until I can get away from here as fast as possible to save myself from getting raided and arrested. Before I can leave Briggstown, I have the miserable job of trying to remove all signs of the evil and dirty deeds I committed here but I knew that wouldn't be possible. I had hoped to live and work here for the rest of my life, but that's not feasible anymore. I think I'm being watched so I will take another long break to take all proper precautions and do what I must do.

I must have been negligent somehow, somewhere, which drew suspicion from someone who said something to someone else, or he or she went to the police with their suspicion or observation. Maybe one of my overnight guests heard a scream or a loud noise they didn't understand coming from the 2nd floor. Maybe someone smelled something. I'm desensitized to horrific smells, so I don't usually notice them. But maybe someone came into the front desk and smelled death before I had a chance to thoroughly clean up a recent murder scene. I may never know who ratted me out or how the police got a whiff of my tracks. A person walking their dog may have had a glimpse of me wheeling Ella to the hearse, or maybe it was someone I rejected accommodations, so they called the police for revenge. I'll never know. I'm assuming eventually, the cops will put 2+2 together and raid the Blue Pine. I want to be long gone before that happens. The lab will do research on the garbage bags and body parts to try to identify the victims and the killer. I did my best to clean my tracks, but anyone can make a mistake. I must play it cool until I can get away from here as fast as possible to save myself from getting raided and arrested.

I will surely miss my Blue Pine home because it is terribly sad for me to leave all my brilliant creations and divine décor that served me well for over two incredible years. I had hoped to live and die in Briggstown. Moving away from here has become paramount for my survival, and I will do it. I had pondered that decision for months, since the 1955 holidays. During that time, I reviewed my diploma and made a life choice that would appear sane and completely incognito compared to my time in Briggstown. My life will never be the same again. Nothing will ever compare to my years at the Blue Pine Guests Inn. Nothing ever will. Nothing.

CHAPTER 33

THE PERFECT STORM

I fled from Briggstown in a panic and quandary. I had to get out of this buzzing town immediately to start a new career elsewhere under a new alias and changing my appearance. I shaved off my beard, put on an old pair of slacks and a warm, casual jacket, grabbed my two bags and slipped out the back door. I think I missed the police raid on the Blue Pine by a mere few days. I took the hearse and disappeared into the wee hours of the morning, around 4:00 A.M. while it was dark and Briggstown was still asleep.

I drove south thinking, worrying and cautiously on the lookout for a place to ditch my sentimental, beautiful hearse. I knew I couldn't keep that fine piece of memories because it would be too easily recognized. I was on the run from being prosecuted in a high-profile case, the likes of which the Pine Tree State had never seen. I was positive this route would take me past Bucksport and south onto a lonely back road to a small town out in the country called Vassalboro. I was hopeful to regrettably abandon my hefty hearse somewhere in that insignificant, out-of-the-way country village, then walk until dawn until I could hitch a ride with a farmer or delivery truck driver headed to Waterville. I figured some nice fellow would want to help a lost soul carrying two pieces of luggage. This wasn't a great plan, but I had no choice.

The time had come; I had to rely on my university degrees and get an adjunct professor's teaching position at a college somewhere in New England but far away from Briggstown. I was thirty-five, so I didn't expect much of a problem getting a job. My university days prepared me for another lifestyle change as a backup should I need it if my luck in Briggstown ran out. My chosen alternative profession had several employment options. Luckily, I kept a good rapport with Mr. Price during my years at the Blue Pine, so I was able to swiftly and peacefully sell and close on my Victorian mansion within a few weeks. An ambitious, new out of school, young man wanted to buy a funeral parlor in the Briggstown area. It was an unbelievable coincidence that this weird looking lad came looking to buy when I needed to sell.

His name was Tim Scarry. His skin was as pale as the Queen's with dark, tight curly hair, black framed glasses with thick lenses, a starched white shirt, a green bow tie and baggy grey slacks. He looked like someone auditioning for a character role in a geek movie. With the name Scarry, he was perfect for the job of an undertaker. He surely chose an appropriate career path with his name and weird looks. I had to chuckle to myself, if he only knew what he bought used to be a house of torture and murder, not just a house of death.

I had been winding down a bit with my duties and responsibilities at the Blue Pine before the town's authorities were tipped off. I can only guess what is being said about the strange proprietor that operated the odd Victorian guest house. I had been contemplating before the warning it was time to make a location change. A nosey neighbor, though living across the street, was getting too curious about my shady operation. That old maid was a busybody. She had come to my door several times in the past few months to borrow a variety of things such as a cup of sugar or a screwdriver. Once she asked for a pair of rubber gloves. I thought that was strange. I was barely polite but stern and turned her away every time without what she came for. Maybe it was her revenge that alerted the police.

I had made up my mind after the holidays to leave the guest home business and embark on a profession that my college education would make possible. I had moved to a new location and changed my profession twice already, staying ahead of the police. I had gotten easily acclimated to a new environment and living a different double life, so I was confident I could do it again, optimistically for the last time.

I had a weird feeling deep down inside me that this next move would be my last, it would be the end of the road for me. Subconsciously at first, I was comparing my crazy double life to Dr. Henry Howard Holmes who was active only three years (1891-

1894) in his murder castle before he was brought down. One year later he was tried, convicted, and hung at the young age of 34 years old. Lately, this has been a conscious thought, because coincidentally, I had operated my murder mansion for less than three years before the police started to look my way. Difference with my situation, I was fortunate to have warnings and I took heed, maybe not soon enough, but I've been lucky.

A gut feeling, the next phase of my life will be my last. I'm young, but I've lived a complex, intense and daring life. I was a successful, prolific murderer for over thirteen years, but I knew my luck couldn't last forever in my murder mansion. I'm sure I will continue killing until I'm caught, killed or die. But now I'm moving to another location for a different line of work. I cannot be Andrew Webb anymore, nor can I be a bearded, Englishman wearing Victorian attire. My appearance will be like the average, 'Joe Schmoe' with a clean-shaven face and my wardrobe will consist of traditional suits and ties.

I'm looking forward to seeing outrageous newspaper headlines and articles around Maine and New England after they find what I had to leave behind at the Blue Pine Guests Inn. I can't imagine all the sinister gossip and dreadful rumors at the Long Drink bar. Worse will be the ultimate shock to Mr. Price when he hears what I had been doing at the Blue Pine. Because time was limited, I felt I was being watched, so I had to leave almost everything behind except for a large suitcase of suits, a duffle bag of my favorite medical tools and of course I wouldn't leave my invaluable pillow, my precious Jackie.

CHAPTER 34

INNKEEEEPER VS. PROFESSOR

It's 1957 now, almost one year since I deserted Briggstown. Today, sitting alone and recalling to mind what happened in '56, I decided to pick up my journal and start writing again, catching up from when I had stopped writing. While I was busy trying to clean up the second floor, selling the Blue Pine and packing items I couldn't leave behind, I did a lot of soul searching to where I would move and what stable career I wanted to take on. I had hitched a ride with a semi-truck driver who was headed down to southern Maine where I once lived.

I considered myself fortunate when I learned in 1956, the American Board of Pathology had recognized forensic pathology as a medical subspecialty, but jobs in Forensic Science were few. In 1957, the American Academy of Forensic Science was founded which helped establish forensic science as a legitimate field of study. Coincidentally, the field I was most interested in had just started to become popular. I had looked for a job that would include aiding criminal investigations by collecting, identifying, classifying and analyzing physical evidence at crime scenes. I figured I'd be good at crime scene investigation, because of my experience with dad plus my education. One option was to be a professor of forensic science. In 1955, the University of California, in Los Angeles had established a program in forensic science but that was too far away, and I didn't want to leave Maine. I had become accustomed to the laid-back way of life and the genuine folks who lived here.

I moved back to southern Maine, near Portland again. I had read there were 14 colleges and universities within a 30-mile radius of Portland. I changed my name to Wade Wilson, something short, English and easy to remember. I landed a job as a professor at a college in southern Maine and started doing research in the field of forensic science. I dug my heels into this new profession and lifestyle in order to become proficient in living another double life.

Within a few months, I bought a small, economical car and started traveling to universities and colleges around southern Maine as a guest speaker presenting educational lectures at conferences and classes. My topic is Forensic Pathology which is pathology that focuses on determining the cause of death by examining a corpse. I've also developed an interest in body farms.

I became well-known in this field of education and highly respected by my colleagues in the field, police officers, other officials in law enforcement and folks in the judicial system. Most everyone I met had heard about my lectures and praised me for my detailed knowledge. A male student was joking with me after class one day and said,

"Professor Wilson, you speak to us with such authentic, intense emotion and extraordinary details that it almost sounds like you were the killer! Isn't that a trip?"

When Philip said that to me, I had to hide my distress and laugh with him, but inside I was stunned and speechless, so I just giggled with false amusement and bid him a goodbye for the day. I knew I was an exceptional speaker, but whoa, I never expected a comment like that.

In more detail, I speak to groups and classes about solving crimes, both unsolved, cold cases and current, recent homicides. I'm also hired for trials as an expert witness. I teach from an academic perspective laced with my personal experiences which makes my presentations overwhelmingly interesting and notable. The good word about me got around fast, so I've been busier than ever before. At first, I thought I wouldn't have enough time for my extra-curricular activities, but sooner than I expected, everything worked out to my advantage. I hugged Jackie every day and slept with her every night. Within a year, I was headed for a satisfactory, double life once again.

Each time I give a presentation about a homicide, especially about a murderer, I re-lived an experience I had as I discussed the gory details of each horrific crime. By explaining the crimes in explicit details, I get incredible sexual stimulation where sometimes I have to hide my hands in my jacket or slacks pockets or under the desk so no one would see them shaking. Sometimes, I have to refrain from speaking because my stutter becomes more noticeable when I'm nervous or excited. There have been a few times, I couldn't refrain from rubbing or squeezing myself under my desk or behind the podium from which I speak. My desires fire up for a little gratification in public, however private. It's always a thrill to feel excited when I talk and the fear of a student detecting my abhorrent thoughts and/or suppressed behavior. I can't afford to lose this job or my outstanding reputation because this is the perfect coverup for my extracurricular activities off campus.

CHAPTER 35

ANDREW WEBB'S TESTAMENT

Not knowing when the last time I will be able to write in my journal, I want to document a brief summary of my life and why I decided to keep a journal. Because of my inimitable experience and extensive education, I considered my journal would hold a wealth of knowledge and information that would be valued data to educators and researchers in the fields of Forensic Science, Clinical Forensic Psychology, Pathology and Criminal Justice to name only a few. I may never earn the exalted fame of other murderers, but the contents of my journal could be seen to have a lasting, influential impact of educational value for future generations. Therefore, my journal is My Legacy.

I'm a psychopathic, sexual sadist, necrophiliac, pedophile and ruthless murderer. I write about myself and my life. I have detailed an up close and personal look at how I think, how I feel and why I love my life and my work. Undeniably, I'm a cruel and violent monster who has no control of my impulses or evil desires.

I realized before puberty I was not normal when I realized I was fascinated with roadkill. Seeing dead, bloody animals perked my curiosity to the point, I wanted to kill them myself. First, I dissected my goldfish, then I tortured the neighbor's cat. I hung it by the neck on a tree in their back yard.

One year went by but my fantasies and yearning to kill animals surfaced again when I started to masturbate. I joined in circle jerks with a couple of other boys my age behind our garage, or behind other buildings, but my buddies would always talk about girls while my thoughts were deviant and not shared. From that first exhibitionistic experience, I was convinced I was different from the rest. I've lived with the anxiety of feeling alone and looking strange to my peers. I have been plagued with bizarre fantasies since I was six years old.

Being born and raised in a funeral home and spending countless hours in the embalming chamber and the morgue must have predisposed me for my deviant sexuality and paraphilias, although, I was showing psychopathic signs of violent tendencies and antisocial personality disorder before six years old, but I will leave my diagnosis to the psychiatrists in this field.

Fortunately, I was a smart kid with above average intelligence. Our family doctor told my parents he guessed my I.Q. was somewhere between 150 - 160. I didn't pay any attention to that, I just felt it was easy to breeze through high school with good grades. I started doing research in the public library when I was thirteen. My main interest was to find out what professions would be most suited for my career considering my bizarre sexual desires. Therefore, I applied to a university that was noted for the academic courses I needed.

At seventeen, I graduated high school with honors and earned a scholarship to NYU to study Forensic Science, Pathology and Forensic Psychology. Forensic scientists examined and analyzed evidence from crime scenes, etc., to develop objective findings that assist in investigations, profiles and prosecutions of criminals or to absolve innocent persons from suspicion. Forensic psychology teaches an overview of the causes of crime and criminal behavior. I figured these courses would be of great interest and possibly lead to an educational career for me in the future if it became necessary. I was impressed to learn professions associated with degrees in these courses of study would bring high paying salaries. I would fit in contentedly. I couldn't predict the future.

I knew I wouldn't be disturbed by the physical or emotional effects of these jobs because killing animals didn't faze me at six years old. Viewing victim's severely torn apart from fatal car accidents or decomposed corpses wouldn't bother me after living in a funeral home and working in a morgue. I saw some bodies in horrific, grizzly condition, disfigured faces, guts hanging out all over, anything you could or couldn't imagine. I have lived in what some people would call a daily horror show, but nothing bothers me.

What is still a mystery to me is why don't I have much control of my sexual desire?. Why will I always have to live a life of agony before the ecstasy?

I never felt any empathy for the dead or their loved ones nor remorse for those I've killed, raped and tortured to death. I had considered becoming a university professor, or a forensic medical examiner, preferably a medical examiner so I could work in a morgue. But I was aware that one of the pros of being a forensic psychologist, also known as a criminal profiler, would be working with law enforcement. I liked that, so I could be aware and informed of the status of criminal investigations. Conversely, because I was still young, I thought it was to my advantage to become a professor at a university first, for a few years. During that time, I brushed up on forensic psychology, related subjects and achieved a notable reputation. Soon, I figured I would be able to seek employment for my more desired occupation.

CHAPTER 36

THE DEAD END

I was admired in the world of academia in Maine. My lectures on anatomy drew packed auditoriums. Students and professors alike clung to my words as though every sentence revealed the secrets and mysteries of life itself. My British accent drew a lot of attention especially from the female scholars. My deep, smooth voice expressed culture, confidence and wisdom. My extensive knowledge brought me overnight fame because no one knew the truth that my fascination with death and human anatomy was not academic. It was intimate.

Every night in the silence of the university, I continued to pursue my passionate studies. The morgue had always been my sanctuary, and the cadavers were my true companions. While everyone else saw cold, dead flesh and medical waste, I saw beauty and solace in stillness and obedience in silence. In death, there was no judgement, only devotion.

Not long after my esteemed employment was established, whispers had begun. Fame always attracts unfavorable attention, envy and sometimes danger which were all pertinent to my line of work. Rumors started circulating on how long and why I lingered in the morgue. Some remarks I heard whispered in the halls were about how strangely I touched the cadavers during demonstrations. In the beginning, the students appeared to be joking frivolously, but as time went on, the gossips spread to the staff, and they started watching me, then it took an ugly turn.

That same week, I heard a janitor reported hearing odd noises and muffled groans in the dead of night, while sweeping the hallway near the morgue. He didn't go into the morgue because of his superstitions, so there was no proof of his claims which could not be explained, nor substantiated. The hearsay died down, so the administration dismissed it, saying the charming, Professor Wilson was indeed eccentric, but certainly brilliant. That was a close call.

I couldn't let myself be bothered by anything said about me or unreliable rumors roaming around the campus, because I knew famous people were liked and disliked equally. However, I felt in my heart the end for me was coming and soon the dark side of the truth would engulf me. I wasn't scared. I was uneasy. Did other infamous killers fear being caught and making headlines? I purposefully changed my line of work from innkeeper to professor, to evade being arrested in Briggstown, but I could not change my true self or my sexual desires. Fortunately, I had found another profession to be near the dead where I have my comfort zone.

It was time. I questioned myself. Was I being paranoid? No. Did the close call trouble me more than I realized? Not sure. Did I want my final days to be spent in captivity being degraded and dictated to by the judicial system and prison guards? Absolutely not. I idolized Herman Webster Mudgett AKA H.H. Holmes, but a legendary person deserved better than imprisonment suffering on death row until he was hanged. My objective is not to look like a copycat of Holmes. I want my life's finale to be different from him and from all others.

I have never wanted anyone to dominate me; hence this is why I have passion for the dead. No one can be more submissive and disciplined than a corpse. Therefore, I won't let anyone put me behind bars, even if it came with more fame. I had something better in mind.

Today, there is a big storm coming. It rattled the windows of the university as I write. I welcome the background sound in the silence of my privacy. Tonight, I will write in my journal prior in time before descending into the morgue once more. It was way past everyone's bedtime, the halls deserted, except the echoes of my boots. I carried a bottle of laudanum mixed with something darker, something final with my secret journal and photographs in the other hand. I have prepared my drink as carefully as a surgeon's cut. It will be nice to have a relaxing cocktail in the most peaceful place on earth.

In the morgue, I opened a drawer, revealing the body of a young woman awaiting dissection in the morning by the medical students. Her skin was pale, stretched taut under the fluorescent light and her lower body was a bluish purple. She was not a beautiful specimen, but a bride not to be.

'You understand me. You will never leave me,' I mumbled with tenderness and also wrote it down.

I drew the corpse into my arms, cradling her cold torso against my warm chest and rocking gently side to side as in a lover's embrace. Then, with a theatrical display, like a lecturer demonstrating the conclusion of an experiment, I uncorked the bottle. Out loud and with conviction, I spoke.

'To life, to death, to silence.'

The poison burned as it slid down his throat. He laid back down on the slab beside the corpse and pulled it close. Andrew's vision swirled; the ceiling lights blurred into halos, his body shook, then he fell back down on the slab as he pressed his lips against the dead girl's cheek for one last meaningful kiss.

Hours later, the morning staff found Andrew and his journal in which he wrote down his end in life. The great professor Wilson, scholar of anatomy, lay stone-dead in the morgue, his face twisted into a grotesque smile and his arm wrapped tightly around the female cadaver in blissful, eternal possession. The bottle lay shattered on the floor, its contents gone.

The university hushed the scandal. They called it a "tragic collapse under the weight of his genius." After the journal was retrieved, the truth seeped out in whispers at first, student passing rumors and adding their curious comments. The janitor, repeating the details of what he had heard, then all the grave details mentioned in the journal became the talk of the town which spread through New England like an out-of-control wildfire. Wade Wilson was Andrew Webb so it was Andrew's notable reputation that rotted as his corpse did and though justice never touched him, his end became a legend.

For years, students swore the morgue was haunted. They claimed sometimes during dissection, they could feel Professor Wilson's eye upon them and hear his calm voice whispering in the silence:

"The dead never judge… they only wait."

Stories are just stories, but Andrew's suicide enraged the people in town for not having been told the truth and how and why a fine man, like Professor Wilson had suffered unconceivably. It made no sense and left an unrest, but in reality Andrew Webb, former Innkeeper and Professor got away with all the brutalities and murders he was responsible for. Even his death was controlled by him.

THE LETTER

'Sealed in an Envelope – Addressed to a Newspaper.

Found at the End of Andrew's Journal.'

Dear Editor,

I would like to introduce myself. My name is Andrew Webb.

For some family history, my first ancestors originated in France but settled in England in the late 19th century. My parents were both immigrants from England in 1920. As adolescents, both mum and dad arrived in the United States in the same boat and entered New York City through the Castle Garden depot. They met on the ocean journey, had a brief courtship, and married soon after arriving on American soil. They first settled in the Lower East Side of NYC in the East Village. A few months later when money was running out for food and rent, dad read in the New York Times about a live-in position working at a funeral home in upstate New York. The ad said, "on the job training", so my dad took the challenge and applied. The owner and mortician liked my dad's enthusiasm, so he approved of lodging for both of my parents and a paycheck for dad. This was a perfect situation as my mum was seven months pregnant with me at the time.

My life story is a complex, deviant and nerve-wracking drama. You'll see, I've lived a double life like most murderers, and I realized I am most like two of them, John Christie, a British serial killer who operated during my time and H.H. Holmes who I read about who operated in the 1890s. Many readers won't believe everything I have put in print, yet others will see my life story as repulsive, dark, and criminal which it is. If my journal is ever found, some people may enjoy reading about my life. I've known since I was a young boy, I was different from my peers, and I never fit in. My classmates never liked me, nor wanted to be friends, sensing there was something odd and mysterious about me.

I was born in that funeral home on the bitter, windy eve of October 31st, 1921. If you think my birthdate was a curse, to make my childhood more jinxed, I grew up in a funeral home under a strict religious, Christian mother who read the Bible to me every day. I did not like hearing the same stories repeatedly, so it made no sense to me. Dad didn't care about religion. His only dedication was to the corpses in the basement. I didn't know the wherefore, nor did I know what his dedication encompassed.

My journal will reveal in my own words, how, why and when I started my evil ways, how I progressed needing more and getting more deranged over time. I wanted to tell the world why and how I became a notorious serial murderer. If my experiences weren't told from my mouth, it would only be heard as another evil, misunderstood story, passed around in local bars.

I'm aware my true-life story is one to be studied by the best academic professors, researchers and mental health experts in psychology, sexology, sociology and forensic sciences. Someday, long after I'm dead and buried I have no doubt a movie, book or a documentary will be made from my journal which is also my autobiography. Frankly, I wish it happened before my demise so I could see it on the silver screen myself. But like most blockbuster movies, there is a thrilling ending, so if I'm still alive, or in prison, there wouldn't be a gripping ending.

I have written this journal in both present and past tense. Sometimes I wrote before I did my dirty deed, frequently during an uncontrollable experience and other times my report came soon afterwards. Remember this. I achieve my supreme source of joy and sexual pleasure watching and listening to my victims' cry out in pain and anguish. I get my thrills by violently torturing and killing living things. I don't always understand myself or my sick desires, so I documented my most horrendous experiments, most horrific methods and psychopathic homicides for the professionals in these fields to analyze.

I may go down in history as the most prolific, sexually sadistic killer of all time. Personally, I would be honored for that recognition.

Sincerely,

Andrew Webb

THE END

GLOSSARY

1- Wikipedia Online Encyclopedia
Wikipedia.org & Other Online Research

- Arsenic Poisoning – Wikipedia. https://en.wikipedia.org/wiki/Arsenic_poisoning

- H.H. Holmes – Wikipedia
https://www.bing.com/search?q=H.H.+Holmes+Gas+Chamber

- Electric Chair – Wikipedia
https://en.wikipedia.org/wiki/Electric_chair

- Guillotine – Wikipedia
https://en.wikipedia.org/wiki/Guillotine

- Category: Medieval Instruments of Torture – Wikipedia
https://en.wikipedia.org/wiki/Category:Medieval_instruments_of_torture

- House of Mirrors – Wikipedia
https://en.wikipedia.org/wiki/House_of_mirrors

- Pedophilia – Wikipedia
https://en.wikipedia.org/wiki/Pedophilia

- Paraphilia – Wikipedia
https://en.wikipedia.org/wiki/Paraphilia

- Serial Killer – Wikipedia. https://en.wikipedia.org/wiki/Serial_killer#
Forensic Pathology – Wikipedia. https://en.wikipedia.org/wiki/Forensic_pathology

- [Casket vs Coffin: 7 Key Differences, Pricing, & More (wikihow.com)](#)

https//www.wikihow.com/Casket-vs-Coffin

- Hanging in the United States – Wikipedia

https://en.wikipedia.org/wiki/Hanging_in_the_United_States

- Writer's block. https:// en.wikipedia.org/wiki/Writer%27s_block
- Symphony by Rachmaninoff. https://en.wikipedia.org/wiki/Isle_of_the_Dead_(Rach maninoff)

- Avon Products – Wikipedia. https://en.wikipedia.org/wiki/Avon_Products

2- What Is Embalming? A Guide to the Embalming Process. January 12, 2023

www.funeralguide.co.uk/help-resources/arranging-a-funeral/funeral-guides/wha…

3- The Embalming Process: How It Works . March 22, 2019

https://www.legacy.com/advice/the-embalming-process-how-it-works

4- TheSmartLocal Singapore

TheSmartLocal is part of TSL Media Group www.funeralguide.co.uk/help-resources/arranging-a-funeral/funeral-guides/wha…

5- Britannica

History & Society . embalming

Written and fact-checked by The Editors of Encyclopedia Britannica

http://www.britannica.com/topic/embalming . Last Updated: Article History. Jul 20,1998

6- Autopsy/History, Procedure, Purposes, & Facts

https://www.britannica.com/topic/autopsy

7- HowStuffWorks . 5 Things You Didn't Know About
Autopsies . January 1, 1970
https://www.science.howstuffworks.com/5-things...

8- The Electric Chair / Torture Museaum
torturemuseum.net/en/the-electric-chair/

9- The Castle – H.H. Holmes: Master of Illusion – Crime
Library
https://crimelibrary.org/serial_killers/history/holmes/11.htm
by Kathryn Ramsland

10- The Most Painful Medieval Torture Devices Ever Used .
November 9, 2023
https://allthatsinteresting.com/medieval-torture

11- Discover Walks Blog. 15 Insane (but true) Facts about the
French Guillotine
(discoverwalks.com) July 10, 2022

12- Proust and the Sex Rats / The New Yorker
http:// www.newyorker.com/culture/cultural-comment/proust-
and-the-sex-rats
By Adam Gopnik . June 13, 2021

13- Funeral Home Supplies and Equipment – lynchsupply.com
http://www.lynchsupply.com/FUNERAL_Equipment_Supplies
_s/86.htm

14- MortuaryMall.com: Funeral Home, Crematory, Autopsy,
and Morgue Equipment & Supplies . morturarymall.com

15- Necktie Party Definition & Meaning – Merriam-Webster
https://www.merriam-webster.com/dictionary/necktie%20party

16- The Ultimate Guide To Victorian Décor – House Digest

https://www.housedigest.com/825907/the-ultimate-guide-to-victorian-decor/

17- Victorian Men's Fashion History and Clothing Guide
https://vintagedancer.com/victorian/victorian-mens-fashion-history/

18- Phrasefinder – the Oxford Dictionary:
https://www.phrases.org.uk/bulletin_board/59/messages/219.html

19- https:// www.bing.com/search

20- https:// www.psychologytoday.com/us/blog/wicked-deeds/201406/origin-the-term-serial-killer by Scott A. Bonn Ph.D. – June 9. 2014

21- Crime Museum – H.H. Holmes. https://
https://www.crimemuseum.org/crime-library/serial-killers/hh-holmes

22- HistoricalCrimeDetective.com.
https:// www.historicalcrimedetective.com

23- Cake – History of Cremation in the United States by Sam Tetrault, BA in English. https://
www.joincake.com/blog/history-of-cremation/ 10/29/2021

24- News-Medical.net   Hip Replacement History by Dr. Ananya Mandal, MD
https:// www.news-medical.net/health/Hip-Replacement-History.aspx 6/10/2023

25- https://symbolgenie.com/origin-of-word-forensic-meaning/

26- DigitalCommons@UMaine

"Information Regarding the Maine State Prison, Thomaston, Maine 1824-19 . . ." by Allan L. Robbins (umaine.edu) https://digitalcommons.library.umaine.edu/mainebicentennial/123/

27- Average Joe – Wikipedia. https://en.wikipedia.org/wiki/Average_Joe

28- Bachelor's Degree . https://www.coursera.org/articles/how-long-does-it...

29- Forensic Science. https://www.bing.com/search?q=what+colleges+taught+forensic+science+in+1957%3F&q

30- https://www.mentalfloss.com/article/69445/43-charmingly-odd-british-town-names

31- https://www.bing.com/search?q=when+did+the+term+signifigant+other+come+out&qs=n&form

32- httpwww.betterhelp.com/advice/memory/difference-between-eidetic-memory-and-photographic-memory/s:// Updated 12/15/2023 by BetterHelp Editorial Team

33- British Slang. https:// foreignlingo.com/british-slang-for-girl/

34- 6 Best Bourbons https://www.liquor.com/best-bourbon-old-fashioned-8401279

35- Anatomy of Love. https://theanatomyoflove.com/blog/courtship/5-stages-courtship/#google_vignette

36- Women's fashions in 1950s. https://vintagedancer.com/1950s/womens-1950s-pants-history/

37- Vintage Dancer. https://vintagedancer.com/1950s/1950s-hairstyles/

38- British Expressions.
https://www.fluentu.com/blog/english/british-expressions//

39- Modus operandi. https://www.merriam-webster.com/dictionary/modus%20operandi

40- Old British sayings:
https://www.bing.com/images/search?q=British+English+Slang&form=RESTAB&first=1

https://www.bing.com/images/search?q=1940s+british+sayings+and+slang&qpvt=1940s+British+sayings+and+slang&form=IGRE&first=1

41- 1902 SearsRoebuck Co., Inc. Catelog. https://www.mentalfloss.com/article/32287/11-bizarre-and-dangerous-items-sold-sears-1902
Arcenic Poisoning.
https://www.medicalnewstoday.com/articles/241860

42- Embalming. https://www.britannica.com/topic/embalming/Development-of-modern-embalming
https://www.legacy.com/advice/the-embalming-process-how-it-works/#google_vignette

43- Victorian Death Practices.
https://www.bing.com/search?q=victorian+death+practices&FORM=SHOPZR

44- Tea Party. https://www.bing.com/shop?q=Formal+Tea+Party+Menu&FORM=QSRE8

45- Serial Killers.

https://www. crimeandinvestigation.co.uk/article/the-10-most-prolific-serial-killers-in-modern-history

46- How Long Does Embalming Last? Everything You Should Know | Cake Blog (joincake.com); https:/ /www.joincake.com/blog/search//

47- DSM-5-TR: https:/ www.psychiatry.org/psychiatrists/practice/dsm

48- https://www.funeralwise.com/cremation/cremation-process/

49- https://psychopathsinlife.com/how-psychopaths-choose-groom-their-victims/

50- Brit Slang in the Bedroom & Related to Sex: https://anglotopia.net/site-news/featured/brit-slang-british-slang-bedroom-big-   list-71-british-english-words-related-sex/

51- Heroin- Gilded Age Medicine: Why Ordering Heroin from the Sears Catalog Was A Step Up – Jennifer Hallock https://jenniferhallock.com/2020/12/07/gilded-age-medicine/

52- Morgue Technicians VS. Pathology Assistants: https://woman.thenest.com/morgue-technicians-vs-pathology-assistants-22844.html

53- Prostitution in New York City: Holy Ground: New York City's Red Light District During the American Revolutionary War – Revolutionary War Journal

54- schizophrenia. https://www.merriam-webster.com/dictionary/schizophrenia https://psychcentral.com/schizophrenia/schizophrenia-age-of-onset

55- Quotes. 16 H.H Holmes Quotes to Chill Your Bones | Kizaz Murder Castle - H.H. Holmes, Chicago World's Fair & Layout | HISTORY https:// en.wikipedia.org/wiki/H._H._Holmes

56- British Slang For Whore: Unlocking The Colorful Language Of The UK (learningandliving.net)
https://learningandliving.net/20-british-slang-for-whore/

57- John Christie (serial killer).
https://en.wikipedia.org/wiki/John_Christie_(serial_killer)

58- https://www.oxygen.com/mark-of-a-serial-killer/crime-news/why-do-serial-killers-take-souveniers

59- The Psychological Profiling of Serial Killers: Inside the Criminal Mind - CrimPsy: August 15, 2025 by ayoubchaaba12@gmail.com

60- Speaking of Psychology: Understanding the Mind of a Serial Killer
Episode 281, with Louis Schlesinger, Ph.D.
61- Delving into the Psyche of Serial Killers: simplyforensic.com

62- "Love looks not with the eyes, but with the mind..." Quote - Shakespeare

63- Cyanide | Chemical Emergencies | CDC
www.cdc.gov/chemical-emergencies/chemical-fact-sheets/cyanide.html

64- List 25. Most Monstrous Serial Killers of Children in History.
https:// list25.com/25-monstrous-serial-killers-of-children/

65- Coffins VS. Caskets. https://www.wikihow.com/Casket-vs-Coffin#
Co-authored by David I. Jacobson and Amber Crain

66- Mickey Finn drink: a surreptitiously drugged alcoholic beverage.
https://en.wikipedia.org/wiki/Mickey_Finn_(drugs) Also in Definitions.

67- Plastination: a technique to preserve a body.
https://en.wikipedia.org/wiki/Plastination

68- Giants of Orthopaedic Surgery: Austin T. Moore MD
https://pmc.ncbi.nlm.nih.gov/articles/PMC5085962/

69- Extreme Embalming. https://allthatsinteresting.com/extreme-embalming

70- American Casket Coffins –
https://www.comparethecoffin.com/american-casket-coffins/

71- Extreme embalming for lengthy preservation.
https://copilot.microsoft.com/chats/JbU6VqiQLVrWSemaVxb1S

Definitions

1- Definition of a paraphilia and 'paraphilic desires':
A **paraphilia** is a condition in which a person's sexual arousal and gratification depend on fantasizing about and engaging in sexual behavior that is atypical and extreme. A paraphilia is considered a disorder when it causes distress or threatens to harm someone else. www.psychologytoday.com/us/conditions/paraphilias

2- squiffy – slang for tipsy or drunk.
https://foreignlingo.com/british-slang-for-drunk/

3- bollocks – male testicles. Brit Slang: https://anglotopia.net (Information for a lot of Brit. slang in the 'Innkeeper'.)

4- pipe sniftner. Also known as a tulip glass designed for sipping liquors, particularly cognac.

5- Catafalque – https://en.wikipedia.org/wiki/Catafalque

6- Tart, bint, crumpet, hoore, hurdie, sket.
https:// letslearnslang.com/british-slang-for-whore/

7- Shutter nutter – 1950s Slang Words & Phrases Woth Remembering.
   https:/ www.yourdictionary.com/articles/1950s-slang

8- Mickey Finn drink: a surreptitiously drugged alcoholic beverage.
   https://en.wikipedia.org/wiki/Mickey_Finn (drugs)

Crum-a-grackle: is a British dialect word that means perplexity or difficulty often used to express confusion or a challenging situation. https://www. wordsandphrasesfromthepast.com/word-of-the-day/crum-a-grackle

ABOUT THE AUTHOR - BIO

Charlayne E. Grenci, Ph.D. is a clinical sexologist, clinical professor, an author and a relationship expert, a graduate from Maimonides University, an affiliate of The American Academy of Clinical Sexologists and a Diplomat of The American Board of Clinical Sexology.

She is a clinical professor, sex educator and coach, sex scientist, researcher and guest lecturer, formerly with a private practice in Florida. Dr. Grenci specializes in life coaching, sex education and instruction for individuals, couples, or groups who are seeking advice, information and support in order for her clients to improve their sexual relationships, sexual issues or alternative lifestyles. Dr. Grenci is also a specialist in relationship and marriage issues and pre-marital coaching.

Charlayne E. Grenci, Ph.D. has inspired, entertained and educated thousands of people for forty-five years with her knowledge, experience and amazing life's story. Dr. Grenci has written several books, from academic to memoir and fiction and is available for presentations, book signings, as a guest speaker or for seminars, private sessions and special educational courses by E-mail, On-Line Video and Cell.

FOLLOW THE AUTHOR

Website: http://www.drgrenciphd.com/

Website: http://www.drgrenciphd.com/queenofdomination/

Website's Author Page: http://www.drgrenciphd.com/author/

Amazon Page: http://www.amazon.com/Charlayne-Grenci/e/B00MYFLMZG/

Facebook: https://www.facebook.com/GMistress1980

LinkedIn: https://www.linkedin.com/in/charlaynegrenci- ph-d-57a47141

GooglePlus: http://bit.ly/2dqN7ds or + http://bit.ly/25wVjBS

Twitter: https://www.twitter.com/GMCarla or twitter.com/CharlayneGrenci

FetLife: GMistress Carla

https://www.goodreads.com/user/show/43358611-charlayne-grenci-ph-d

CONTACT INFORMATION

Charlayne E. Grenci, Ph.D.

For Information on Private Sessions and Other Inquiries:
E-mail: DrGrenci@bellsouth.net

For Booking of Guest Speaking Engagements' and Book-Signing
Presentations Call: 1-954-980-2780 (2:00 P.M. - 6:00 P.M.)
Monday - Friday, (Eastern Standard Time)

Website: http://www.drgrenciphd.com/

Author page: http://www.drgrenciphd.com/author/

Send Snail Mail for Tributes or to purchase a signed copy of a
book(s):

Dr. C. E. Grenci
P.O. Box 50602,
Lighthouse Pt., FL 33074

Charlayne E. Grenci, Ph.D. has inspired, entertained and educated
thousands of people for forty-five years with her knowledge,
experience and amazing life's story.

AUTHOR'S BOOKS

Author's Books: Hardcovers, Paperbacks and/or E-books by Dr. Grenci

INNKEEPER, JOURNAL DISCOVERED: REVEALING TORTURE MURDERS & ATROCITIES

RECIPES TO DIE FOR, A CRIME NOVEL WITH TRADITIONAL ITALIAN CUISINE +

QUEEN OF DOMINATION: My Secret Life (2014)

AMERICA'S NOTORIOUS DOMINATRIX, Sex, Crime & Punishment (2017) Part One

DARK SIDES of SOCIETY, Forbidden World of Hedonism (2017) Part Two

SECRET CINEMAS, 10 Erotic Movie Fantasies (2016)

SECRETS BEHIND CLOSED DOORS (2017)

SECRET CINEMA, CARNAL CONFESSIONS, Twisted, Lustful, Forbidden Fantasies & Guilty Pleasures (2019)

MARCEL PROUST EXPOSED (2015)

SECRET CINEMAS: LAST CURTAIN FOR A STRIPPER (E-Book Only)

POLITICIAN EXPOSED (E-Book Only)
Links for Ordering: http://www.amazon.com/Charlayne-Grenci-PhD/e/B01MU2H05G

Links - To Author's Books

INNKEEPER, JOURNAL DISCOVERED: REVEALING TORTURE MURDERS & ATROCITIES

RECIPES TO DIE FOR,
Paperback: https://www.amazon.com/dp/
Kindle/E-Book: https://www.amazon.com/dp

QUEEN OF DOMINATION, My Secret Life:
Paperback: https://www.amazon.com/dp/B00NXG4572/
Kindle:
https://www.amazon.com/Queen-Domination-My-Secret-Life/dp/1935752510/

AMERICA'S NOTORIOUS DOMINATRIX, Sex, Crime & Punishment
Paperback:
https://www.amazon.com/dp/1982082585/
Kindle/E-Book:
https://www.amazon.com/dp/B078PXYY6K/

SEQUEL:
DARK SIDES OF SOCIETY, Forbidden World of Hedonism:
Paperback:
https://www.amazon.com/dp/1981527133/
Kindle/E-Book:
https://www.amazon.com/dp/B078BC5ZP5/

SECRETS BEHIND CLOSED DOORS:
Paperback:
https://www.amazon.com/Secrets-Behind-Closed-Charlayne-Grenci/dp/198168459X
Kindle/E-Book: https://www.amazon.com/dp/B078L7RG48/

SECRET CINEMA, CARNAL CONFESSIONS (on AMAZON)
https://www.amazon.com/Secret-Cinema-Confessions-C-Grenci/dp/1935752634
Kindle/E-Book: https://www.amazon.com/Secret-Cinema-Confessions-C-Grenci-ebook/dp/B07Z84WD1Z

MARCEL PROUST EXPOSED:
Paperback: https://www.amazon.com/Marcel-Proust-Exposed-Charlayne-Grenci/dp/1935752596/
Kindle: https://www.amazon.com/Marcel-Proust-Exposed-Charlayne-Grenci-ebook/dp/B011YKLWQK

PHOTO - DR. C.E. GRENCI